CLADDAGH
&C...

CAYCE POPONEA

Cover Design by Mayhem Cover Creations
Formatting by Champagne Formats

Champagne
Formats

ISBN-13 978-1511421409
ISBN 10 1511421401

Other work by Cayce Poponea

Shamrocks and Secrets

Coming summer of 2015 . . .
Crain's Landing

DEDICATION

When the end of Shamrocks and Secrets was in sight, one of my friends asked me why I chose to end it so bluntly. She told me, it was as if you just added water and poof, three kids and a dog. She wanted to know how they got there. Did they spend everyday living life to the fullest? Or did Patrick and Christi face the same harsh realities of life and come out as a stronger, healthier couple? Thus the birth of Claddagh and Chaos. So . . . to my dearest friend, Gemma Warburton. This is for you. I hope you enjoy!!!

Chapter One

HE SOFT PATTERING OF RAINDROPS combined with the gentle, cool breeze had stirred me from my brief but much needed sleep. The feel of Christi's warm, soft body nestled against mine was the only reminder assuring me this was all real. Even with the cool temperature of the room, the sheet she was under barely covered her lower half. I ran my index finger along the outline of her slender spine, caressing the beautiful skin that rested there.

I welcomed the rain; it ensured that my plan for my new wife wouldn't be interrupted by a desire to enjoy the green landscape or any of the other activities the village had to offer. No, today I would keep my Christi right where she was now.

I watched as the breeze ruffled the sheer curtains that adorned the door leading out to the yard. I could hear the sound of the surf as it broke along the rocky shore, the waves crashing over and over, like a lullaby. How I wished we could stay here in our little cocoon for the rest of our lives, no one to interrupt the peace and quiet.

The desire to have her again was overwhelming. Last night was the first time we had been together since prior to the kidnapping. Once I had her in the house, I had thrown her onto the bed and taken what was mine, in turn giving her what was hers.

My hand made contact with the tip of her shoulder, caressing her shoulder blade, down her soft back, finally to the junction of her hip and the two tiny dimples that stood proud like a beacon for my pleasure. It was as I started to make my way back up her spine that the glint from the Claddagh ring on my pinky finger caught my attention. I sighed, remembering how only a day ago, I had made the promise, placing it on my finger.

When I was a boy, my father always made time for me and my sister. He would take me to ballgames or just hang out in the backyard and throw the ball around. With my sister, he would take her out to dinner and show her how men were supposed to treat her.

I could remember one time my father took me out for ice cream. Amex was at a friend's house and so it was only da and me. I remembered seeing his Claddagh ring on his pinky finger, but I never paid much attention to it. So, sitting outside in the heat of June in Chicago watching our favorite team win , I asked my father where he had gotten that ring.

"Patrick, one day in the future, you'll stand in front of all the family and God and make a promise to a beautiful, young girl. You'll promise to protect her, provide for her, and most of all, love only her. But before you do that, you'll stand in front of all the men in our family and you'll swear an oath to always put your family first."

I had nearly forgotten about the ring and story he shared when my father and uncles came into the room as I was dressing for the wedding yesterday. At first, I was worried my nightmare had come true and they were here to tell me she had changed her mind. The look on my father's face was one of severity and seriousness. What happened next was something I would remember for the rest of my life.

"Patrick . . ." His tone confirmed what he was about to say would change my life. "As you know, you're about to take a vow of marriage."

I didn't respond. My job was to listen and listen well. Even if I was about to get married to the most perfect creature to walk the planet, I knew he would have me shot me for less than simple disrespect.

"You know that for generations, the men of this family have made a vow of our own. One we keep among the men of this family."

Behind him stood not only my uncles, but some of my closest men, as well as men from my extended family. Matthew stood beside my father, his look as pensive. Sherman and Caleb stood tall beside him, hands in a stolid stance, faces absent of the traditional smiles.

"You were given the position as the head of this family because of your birth. You're given the gift of being head of your family by sheer luck. Being a husband and father is an honor. One we don't take lightly."

I felt my heart begin to pound in my chest. I had sworn to Christi I wouldn't have my gun on me at our wedding. I was regretting that promise.

"The shamrock you gave to Christi was a promise, but the Claddagh holds so much more."

My memories came flooding back to me of the ring my father wore on his right pinky finger.

"I told you when you were younger this day would come. I didn't tell you what would be expected by the men of your family and what would happen if you choose to break the vow you give to us today."

I watched as all of the men stood behind my father, a united front; they were making their presence in the room as strong as possible. There would be no misunderstandings today.

"By accepting this ring, you accept the consequences of breaking the solemn vow you make to us; as well, to always honor her and your family."

Knowing how our family worked, I didn't have to ask what would happen if I broke this vow. Besides the obvious of losing Christi and any children we had, someone would have to hand out the ultimate punishment.

"By whose hand?" It was my only question.

"Mine," my father spoke, clear and emotionless , as he extended his open hand with the silver Claddagh resting in his palm.

With absolute confidence, I took the ring from his hand and placed it on my pinky. The vow was now made and my fate sealed. If I ever dishonored my bride, my father would be forced to take my life. I was confident I would die a happily married old man.

"Good morning, Husband." Christi's raspy voice brought me back to the present. She would never know of the vow I had taken. Last night after our second round, she held my hand and it was then she noticed my ring. I told her the truth; that it was a gift from my father.

"Actually, I think it's afternoon."

Covering her body with mine, once again, my need for her was evident against her silky thigh. I learned early on that Christi loved it when I nibbled on the junction of her neck and shoulder. The moan that escaped her vocal cords went directly to my groin, increasing my desire for her.

Christi knew me well, also; she would grab a handful of hair at the back of my neck and tug. That, combined with her sweet moans, would send me to places I had never been. I wanted this feeling to last forever, to make every time I made love to my wife, feel like the first time.

Ignoring her attempt to pull me closer to devour her tempting neck, I pulled myself away. I watched as her confused and dare I say, pissed off face, questioned my action. I pulled the sheet away, eliciting giggles from her. I pressed her hips firmly into the mattress and moved my knees until they were nearly touching her ass cheeks; her knees fell to the side of their own accord. Christi was a beautiful creature, soft and supple, including the glistening lips of her engorged pussy. She called to me, even when she said nothing, her body shouted my name.

"You know, Christi . . ." I leaned my body down, my index finger sliding through the evidence of her arousal. " . . . this is my favorite place on Earth . Here in this bed, with you wide open for me, knowing that in less than ten seconds, I'm going to make you feel so good that you'll forget your name."

My tongue dove into her warm, pink folds. My eyes locked onto the flesh that was created for my sole enjoyment. Christi tried to lift her hips off the mattress as my tongue found its target; her erect clit that was hiding behind the skin protecting it. With the tip of my tongue, I flicked the hardened nub, freeing it from its protective covering. My lips formed a seal as my mouth began to suck. The more she moaned, the harder I sucked. I added first my index finger and then my middle finger, fucking her slowly and methodically with my wet digits. Her fingers were buried deep in my hair, pulling the short strands, causing a pain that I welcomed, encouraging me to go further, love her harder.

"You like that, baby? You like my tongue in your sweet pussy, don't you?" I knew the answer and I knew she was too wrapped in the pleasure I was giving her to do anything but enjoy. I wanted this, craved for her to feel this good and by the things I could do for her. Christi thrusts became more forceful; she was close and wanted more. Her legs began to shake, I moved my mouth away slightly, testing the waters to see her reaction.

"That's it, rub that tight little pussy on my face."

Her head shot up, her hooded eyes glaring at me. She needed control, and I had no issue giving it to her. I moved to lie beside her and pulled her over top of me, bringing her body to straddle my face.

"Put your hands on the head board."

As she reached out for the stained wood, I grabbed her hips, drawing her down onto my tongue. Her cry of pleasure gave me the drive to let her get her fill. She started moving, rising up and down along my erect tongue, tilting her hips on her up-stroke , her clit hitting my nose. Releasing one side of her hip, I moved my thumb to cover her now very swollen clit, circling the wet flesh as her tempo increased. I watched her closed eyes and open mouth, taking great joy in the fact I was giving her such pleasure. Her movements became sloppy and the soft words she was uttering unintelligible.

I knew what was coming, but I wanted to be buried deep inside of her when it happened. I pushed her onto her back; her scream of surprise replaced with a cry of ecstasy as I pushed my hard cock into her tender pussy. I buried myself balls deep in her, loving her, craving her. I wanted to do this everyday, until I took my last breath.

"Patrick, baby . . . yes . . . oh."

Her legs wrapped around me, closing the gap that our bodies created. Grinding her pelvis against mine, giving into her need, taking from me what she needed and giving me so much more. I had to see her, watch as I entered her, rhythmically creating a euphoria that was completely ours. I adjusted my pelvis, raising my torso off her, admiring how her breasts bounced in time with my thrusts. Her nipples were hard and begging to be sampled. Christi, knowing her body as she did, released her grip on my shoulders and placed one on her left tit, while the other traveled south, finding her warm, wet clit. She pulled and pinched her perfect nipples, brushing my cock with her fingers as she pleasured herself. With the combination of her tight pussy walls massaging my cock and the sight of her losing herself in not only the pleasure I was giving her, but the result of her talented fingers against her tender flesh, I found my slice of heaven, thrusting and praying that I could keep this going for days. I watched as my cock entered her over and again, listening to the words that poured from her lips. In the end, as I felt my balls tighten and the coil grow tighter, it was the light reflecting off the diamond ring that sent me over the edge. A ring I had placed on her finger, a sign to the world this amazing woman was mine.

The rain lasted for two days; two wonderful days that we spent naked and wrapped around each other. I felt it was in those two days my son was conceived.

For the next three weeks, we took in all the sights Ireland had to offer. I even took her to the very hillside where I got her shamrock. We walked around the tiny village, spoke with some of the family we still had there, and shopped with several of the merchants who peddled their wares. I learned more about Christi in that time than all the months prior. She had an unhealthy obsession with peanut butter; she had it every morning for breakfast—on her toast and pancakes.

I also found out she had the cutest giggle when she was tickled behind her knee and that she screamed like a little girl when she saw a bug crawl across the floor. I discovered it was very erotic to paint my wife's toenails with nail polish. She discovered that biting gently on my bottom lip made me growl and then attack her. How taking her cup of coffee in the morning was a very bad idea.

I watched as she would twist a piece of her hair around her finger as she read her book. How she hummed an unfamiliar tune when she brushed her teeth. I watched as she laughed wholeheartedly while trying to do cartwheels on the cliff's edge. By the time we had to leave, she had perfected them. Christi was even able to get me to drink 'girlie' drinks only because she made them taste so good.

We learned that even though Hollywood made having sex on a hill side look erotic, it was actually a pain in the ass, literally. You found dirt and grass in places it didn't belong for days afterward.

As we boarded that sea plane heading home, I sighed. I held my gorgeous wife's hand and kissed her forehead, settling into my seat. Christi and I had discussed that once we were back from our honeymoon, our lives would likely become a little crazy. I would have to get caught up with my work and I knew my mother would have something planned for us.

What I didn't know at the time was that my life was about to change in ways I had never dreamed.

Chapter Two

"PATRICK, PLEASE PUT ME DOWN. This is ridiculous." Christi had been demanding that I put her down since we got out of the car.

"Oh, no, I'm nothing if not traditional."

"Yes, but you did this on our honeymoon."

"But we didn't live at that house."

She locked eyes with mine and allowed me to carry her across the threshold of our house. As wonderful as my time alone with her was, I was glad to be home . It was time to start our lives; building a family and raising our children.

It was after midnight when we finally crawled into bed; exhaustion more prevalent than making love to my sleepy wife in our new bed. Christi had taken just enough time to brush her teeth and have a quick shower. She was out before her head hit the pillow.

My mind, however, was in overdrive. I had tons of emails from Caleb and my father. Seems the Feds had started poking their noses in our new ventures in the South. Caleb had been able to reopen some communication with Velinco's old company. It appeared they were more than ready to do business with us. If things went according to plan, both families stood to make a lot of money.

The next morning, I woke to the smell of coffee and something sweet. I turned over to find Christi's side of the bed cold and empty. Once I was showered and dressed, I made my way down the stairs to find my wife in the kitchen. Her hair was pulled into a messy bun atop her head. She was sitting on one of the barstools with her feet dangling down. The book she had started on the flight home was open in her hands. I wanted to take a picture of this moment; have the sight of my wife preserved for all time.

"Are you just going to stare at me all day or are you going to join me for coffee?"

I couldn't help but smile at her. We were very in tune to each other. "I think I'll just watch you."

She set her book down and turned to me. Her smile was enough to make me forget about my day and want to take her back upstairs; show her what watching her did to me.

"Get over here and kiss me." She tried to sound demanding, but she was much too gentle.

"Ask me nicely, Mrs. Malloy."

The look she shot me was one I had seen my ma give my da on many occasions. Closing the distance between us, I tipped my bride back and kissed her breathless. She rewarded me with a nip from her teeth on my bottom lip. Christi was so sexy and sassy, I questioned if I would ever see everything she had to offer or tire of what she consistently gave me. I held the pose as my tongue barged its way into her coffee-flavored mouth, her moan confirming her pleasure and satisfaction. With another kiss to the edge of her neck, I gathered my jacket, adjusted my erection, and winked in her direction as I headed out the door to meet my men.

"So, the crates were open, but nothing was missing?"

Da was sitting to my right and Caleb to my left with Shamus flanking Caleb. It seemed we'd had some interesting break-ins over the past few weeks. The first took place at the docks here in Chicago, the second in Miami.

"Not one fucking thing missing," Sherman responded, the disbelief chambering his attitude.

"Why would . . . ?" Shamus joined Sherman in the confusion line. His eyes told me he was at a complete loss.

"Feds," my father interrupted Shamus. "They just want us to know they're watching." His voice was laced with amusement. Da got a rather big kick out of 'playing' with the guys at the bureau. There were stories upon stories of the things he had done to agents who were on stakeouts. Juvenile things, humorous and, on occasion, costly pranks.

"Well then, you all know what to do."

This wasn't the first time something like this had happened. I also knew, beyond a shadow of a doubt, it wouldn't be the last. I would have my security team place some special equipment in the house and condo, just in case *they* were listening.

"How was the honeymoon, Son? Do we have grandbabies on the way?"

One thing about my da, he was always one to cut to the chase, whether it offended you or not. If he had a question, it was going to get asked.

"Hell, I'm surprised he even showed up this morning. I remember when I first married my Ammo, I didn't get out of bed for days."

Muscles boasted, hugging my shoulder with his clenched fist.

Everyone at the table began to laugh.

"Well, we'll just have to wait and see. Christi stopped taking her birth control before the kidnapping so, with God's blessing, maybe we'll soon have good news." In my family there was no room for secrets. Survival depended on a quick hand and a level head. Having family around you was vital and secrets only created chaos. And chaos was an unwelcome guest . . . it could get you killed.

"You know, Son, the practice is the best part. It might take you a few tries to get it right, you know?"

The very last thing I wanted to hear from my da was talk about sex with my wife. Lucky for me, his wife had placed a huge bug in his ear.

"Oh, before I forget, your mother is insistent on throwing an open house party for you and Christi. She says it would be rude not to invite all your neighbors."

I'd known this was coming and had avoided the subject with Christi. She and I had decided that once we found out she was pregnant, she would stay home with the children. If by chance she was expecting, I didn't want any unnecessary stress to complicate things.

"Do I even want to know what the plans are?" I questioned da.

He only chuckled as he responded, "Well, between your wife and your ma, I have no doubt it'll be wonderful."

As usual, Da was correct. I arrived home that night to find my ma, wife, and sister sitting in the middle of my living room, tossing ideas around like a basketball game.

"Christi, you have to secure the room. Don't have your best china or silver in plain sight; you never know who has sticky fingers. Besides, most of your neighbors will come out of pure curiosity to see what kind of shit you have and if their stuff is better or not." Ma had hosted more of these parties than anyone I knew. She always rented the dishes and glasses; telling my da it was less expensive than replacing the set he had purchased for her as a wedding gift.

"And be prepared for the wives to cling together and talk about how handsome your husband looks." I had to smile at that. Honestly, seeing Christi a little jealous was hot as fuck. Knowing how she would fuck me into oblivion after the last guest left, made me hope my ma was right.

Before I knew it, the date had been set and the invitations mailed. All I had to do was show up, which was particularly easy since I lived there. Ma fluttered around directing the staff Christi had hired, pointing to pieces of furniture that needed to be stored and telling grown men to watch their feet as they carried tables into the room.

Christi appeared with a bunch of grapes in her hand; she had recently developed an obsession for fruit. She always seemed to have a piece in her hand or a bowlful at the ready. So it came as no surprise there were bouquets of it all over our home for our guests to enjoy. I watched with a glint in my eye as she 'sampled' each arrangement for quality.

Honestly, I'd had no idea how many neighbors I had until this very moment. I stood at the edge of the pool, my eyes landing on my glowing wife as she made everyone feel very welcome. She even had special gifts for each of them to take home at the end of the night.

One couple in particular seemed to take a liking to my Christi; Theresa and Clark Johnson. Theresa told us she was an up-and-coming fashion designer. She boasted that she had just signed with several high-end stores and would be selling women's lingerie. She wanted to make women look sexy in and out of the bedroom, yet keep things simple. Thus the name of her line: Simply Theresa. Clark, her husband, was boring as fuck. He stood in my living room, holding a glass of the cheapest scotch I could find, raving about how 'smokey' and 'full bodied' it was. Hell, it was nothing more than watered down iodine. His clothes screamed 'country club reject' and his shoes had tiny pieces of masking tape along the edge. He told us he sold insurance, yet he didn't try to sell any to anyone in the room. This bothered me even more than the eye-fucking he was paying to Christi. There were several powerful men in this room, money clear as day, but he never showed a card or tried to make any contacts.

One by one, the guests began to leave, and I started to make a list of how many ways I was about to violate my new wife. Clark and Theresa informed us they had acquired the house around the corner that had been in foreclosure. Clark raved about how he marched into the bank, slapped down a check, causing angels to fucking sing, and the bank made him customer of the month. In truth, he probably borrowed the money from his rich old granny and had to file her fucking toenails for the rest of her life as restitution.

Once everyone was gone and the house secured, I walked into our room to find my wife slathering on her lotion at the end of the bed. She knew how much I loved to watch her hands massage her tight little body. Almost as much as I liked to watch her pleasure herself. When she was done, she sauntered over to my side of the bed, a small white package dangling from her finger.

"You know, Patrick, everyone got a gift tonight except you." Her voice was seductive and I was certain I was about to get laid. My cock was trying desperately to free himself from my boxers; he knew how well Christi took care of him. She made him feel better than I ever could.

"That's not true, I got you, didn't I?"

Christi was smart as fuck. She knew what to say to get pretty much anything from me that she wanted. I removed my gun from my back holster and placed it on my night stand, never taking my eyes off her now shiny body. I crawled onto the mattress and placed my hands behind my back, giving Christi complete control tonight.

"I actually had something else in mind." She slowly laid the white bag on my bare chest and straddled my hips. "Open it, please."

I smiled as I tore into the delicate tissue paper. Why women spent so much fucking time putting this shit together was beyond me. All that work, and in less than ten seconds it was a crumpled mess on the floor.

As I took the tiny, flat object from the bottom of the bag, I looked at my wife's face. Her bottom lip was strangled between her teeth, her smile still forming and her eyes excited, yet apprehensive.

"Is this what I think it is?"

She smiled and nodded her head, her bottom lip no longer a prisoner to her perfect white teeth.

"You mean . . ." I started, holding the unmistakable stick between us.

Her smile became wider, eyes brighter and her body was vibrating in excitement.

"I'm gonna . . ."

Her excitement reached decibel levels as she brought her hands up to cover her gorgeous lips.

"You're . . ."

"Yes, Patrick, we're having a baby. I'm pregnant."

CHAPTER THREE

Three months later . . .

1 TRACED MY INDEX FINGER across her still-flat stomach, unable to hide the permanent smile plastered on my face. Every night since Christi told me the news of our baby, I had waited until she was fast asleep before my conversations with our little miracle commenced.

At first, there were promises to love him or her unconditionally, to make certain every day was an adventure make time for him or her. Trips to Disney or vacations in the cabin I bought. Just like my wife, there was no limit to what I would do for the child who was growing in her womb.

A month ago, I began to have nightmares. Vivid dreams where I was searching for Christi and our baby, but I couldn't find them. I could hear Christi's laughter and the sweet coos of the baby, but I couldn't find them anywhere. I had awakened several times in a cold sweat. Thank God I had yet to wake Christi. I would never confess them to her, they would only cause her worry. I was more than likely having them due to the added stress I was under.

The shipments that had been found opened were still a mystery; nothing was missing, the boxes were just left open. Da suspected the Feds, but I wasn't so certain. Everyone knew they had a certain protocol they had to follow. Touching evidence was a big no-no in the FBI world. My gut was telling me it was something much worse and my nightmares were confirming that for me.

Several nights found me sitting in one of our warehouses, waiting for whoever was behind this. I could have instructed my men to handle this situation, but the bad feeling I was getting wouldn't leave. So far, I had nothing and that fact alone had me tossing and turning.

It was Wednesday and once more I was sitting in the dark, waiting to see if tonight would be the night I caught the sorry motherfucker red-handed. Angus was beside me; he hadn't said a word or moved a muscle in two hours. He was trained to be in these types of situations, thus the reason I chose him to wait with me. I stood when the need to piss could no longer be ignored. My joints screamed at me for the lack of movement and general exhaustion. I heard movement and stopped dead in my tracks, my Glock in hand, while Angus was already half way across the room. Seconds later a long nose and needy eyes peeked out to reveal it was a rat trying to find food.

I walked down the hall and made my way back to the chair I previously occupied, still needing to piss, but not caring at the moment. I had barely gotten comfortable when Angus spoke.

"Boss?"

"Yeah?"

"I need to ask a favor of ya."

"All right." I closed my eyes for a moment, allowing him the opportunity to say what he needed to say.

"Well, I know I've thanked ye several times for helping me get me citizenship and I feel like a tool for even asking this."

The silence that followed was irritating, to say the least. Angus didn't generally hem and haw around anything. I took a breath and turned to face him as I spoke.

"Angus, I've told you a hundred times, you don't have to thank me. You found my Christi and gave me back my life. You must know I'd do anything you ask of me."

It was quiet for several minutes. Angus wasn't a man of many words; the ones he did voice usually meant something.

"I want to marry me Maggie."

When I was first introduced to Angus he was running from some shit that happened in Ireland. He need a job and a place to live; I gave him both. In return, he had been a faithful and trustworthy advocate. I'd seen him take down men twice his size with a simple hand movement, yet when you placed him in the room with Maggie, he was gentle as a lamb; always making certain she was well cared for and had everything she needed. Maggie had the big lug wrapped tightly around her little finger.

"I've asked her ma and she gave me her blessing. I bought her a ring yesterday. It's nothing like Mrs. Christi's, but my Maggie is a special girl and I want to make the night I propose to her one she will remember."

Listening to Angus speak, reminded me of when I decided I wanted to marry my Christi. How I worried she would say no or laugh in my face. How she would find what I do too much to handle. But, like Maggie, she kept me guessing. I couldn't predict what she would say or how she would react.

"I'd like to borrow your boat so I can take her out and ask for her hand."

"Whenever you're ready, it's yours." I turned and extended my hand to him. "Let me be the first to congratulate you and welcome you to the club." I shook his hand, knowing this was about to change his life. Having someone to come home to every night was one of the greatest feelings I had experienced in my life. Now, God willing, Angus would know that feeling as well.

"Before I forget, have you heard from Tonto lately?"

I settled back in my seat and propped my feet up on the trashcan, crossing my legs at my ankles.

"I saw him this morning at my office. Why?"

Angus took a sip of his coffee, then turned back to face me. "Seems he was over on Ninth Street the other day and went into that little coffee shop on the corner. He heard someone call out his name and turned around to find his high school sweetheart walking toward him."

Angus paused when we heard a noise by the front door. Again, it was a goddamn rat.

"Turns out she was here in Chicago for a job interview. Apparently, he sat down with her and they talked for quite a while. He told me they've picked up where they left off and now she's moving in with him."

"I'm glad to hear that, Angus." Tonto had never had a steady relationship in the time I'd known him. He was a handsome guy, I guessed, and I knew he'd had his fair share of the girls at the club, but never one he called his own.

"Yeah, I told him he was due. Every man should have a reason to go home at night"

I couldn't have agreed more.

The house was quiet as I crept into the kitchen. Christi had left dinner for me in the fridge. I was so hungry I didn't even take the time to put it into the microwave.

After shoveling in the last cold green bean, I rinsed off my plate and placed it into the dishwasher. Even cold, Christi's cooking was amazing.

I double-checked she had locked all the doors and proceeded to set the alarm. My nightmares kept me on alert and made my desire to protect her even greater. As I made my way upstairs, I had to remind myself that only a few feet away lay my wife, snuggled up in our big bed. I couldn't wait to wrap myself around her warm, soft body, finding the one place I called home. Being surrounded by her scent and the feel of her was all I needed to drift off to sleep.

As I opened the bedroom door, I could barely make out her form in the darkness. Christi had to have the room pitch black and the ceiling fan running to be comfortable. I had grown accustomed to stumbling around in the dark so that she was able to sleep.

Standing on my side of the bed, I quietly slipped out of my clothes, but left on my boxers. As carefully as I could, I pulled back the blankets and settled into bed behind my wife. Imagine my surprise when I placed my hand on her stomach to find my Christi completely naked.

"You're home," Christi's sweet voice whispered in the darkness.

"I am, Sweetheart. Shh, go back to sleep, it's early," I whispered in her ear, kissing her neck.

"Mmm . . ." She moaned as she turned in my arms, lying partly on her back. "I have something for you."

Christi placed her hand over mine, slowly moving it to the junction of her thighs. She directed my middle finger to her swollen clit.

"You're not too tired are you?" She questioned as she directed my finger the way she wanted it.

Suddenly, I had all the energy in the world.

"I'm never too tired to make love to you."

Moving my fingers inside her warm, wet walls, I moved my body to hover over hers. I began to lay tender, open-mouthed kisses on her neck and collarbone. Since Christi had become pregnant, her body had started to change. Her breasts had definitely gotten bigger and more sensitive. Her pink nipples had darkened to an erotic shade of red. I was very aware of the tenderness that had also taken over her breasts.

Instead of my usual fevered groping, I now softly circled her nipples with my tongue, while I gently caressed the underside with my fingers. I had stopped nipping at her peaks and only kissed them with my lips and lavished them with the tip of my tongue. She still grabbed the back of my hair and arched her back.

"Umm, now, Patrick."

I only smiled as I continued to rub her clit with my fingers and kiss her nipples. I slowly began to kiss down her body, paying special attention to the area where our baby was growing every day. I would skip our nightly conversation in exchange for a special one with its mother . . . sorry kid.

"Please, Patrick, you can do that next time. I was dreaming about you."

I completely ignored her. Another thing that had changed about Christi since pregnancy was the way her arousal smelled and tasted. I couldn't get enough.

I removed my fingers and spread her lower lips, not pausing for a second before diving in. My chin was immediately coated with her juices, as my fingers worked in rhythm with the lapping of my flattened tongue. I tried to never do the same shit twice, to change things up and keep her begging for more.

"Oh, God!" her voice shouted, as she thrust her hips in the air, shoving my head back slightly.

I held on as I continued my assault, making circles with my tongue around her very swollen clit, causing her legs to shake and powerful moans to escape from her. My fingers played her walls, giving special attention to the rippled skin just inside her pussy.

I knew the moment her climax hit her. Christi wasn't a screamer, but her body always flinched as she came; the way she would still and ride the wave as it rushed over her. She let me continue to coax every contraction out of her orgasm.

I gradually made my way back up her body, but didn't give her a second to say anything before I gently slid into her. Her legs wrapped around my waist as I slid in and out. I knew Christi's body better than I knew my own and I knew what worked for her. I shifted my hips and felt her walls clench around me, which in turn triggered my own climax. I would never tire of making love to my Christi and knew we would always be this way. No words were exchanged as we both drifted off to sleep, naked and blissfully happy.

CHAPTER FOUR

A S I SAT WITH MY men, I methodically pulled my Claddagh ring over my knuckle, slid it back into place, twisted it around twice, then repeated the motions. It was Saturday afternoon, the Red Wings were playing the Chicago Blackhawks, and the score was tied at zero. Books was sitting slumped on the right side of the couch while Caleb was asleep in the reclining chair opposite him, his mouth slightly open, an occasional snore escaping his throat. It was fucking strange how much shit had changed this past year. Since winning over Christi and welcoming her into the family, our lives had done a one-eighty. Once upon a time, I would have been watching this game surrounded by half-naked women, all vying for my attention or bringing me a cold beer on demand. Hell, not a word would have been said if I'd told one of them to get on her fucking knees and suck my dick. I wouldn't disrespect my beautiful wife by doing any of that, no matter how much I silently wanted her to.

Muscles had been watching the two slugs on my couch since the game first began. With a Cheshire grin on his face, he quietly set his beer glass on the bar and made his way over to a now drooling Caleb. All open eyes were on him as he swiftly kicked the recliner, sending the head rest into the wall behind him. Caleb's head bounced once and then it was all over.

"What the fuck . . . ?"

Caleb was quick, even dead asleep, and his .45 was pressed into Muscles's throat, the distinct sound of the gun being cocked echoed in the silent room. Muscles suddenly hit the floor with a loud thud, his arms above his head and Caleb's socked foot in the center of his chest. I couldn't help but laugh at the sight, laugh at what we had become. Lazy assed, married men with nothing better to do than sleep, drink beer, and keep the hell out of our wives' way.

"Dude . . ." Muscles laughed as Caleb helped him off the ground. The loud thud had woken Books and even he was finding amusement with the pair. "Fuckers, what is wrong with you? The game is on and Christi made us mega munchies." He swiped his arm in the direction of the buffet lined up beside the bar. "You can all sleep when you're dead," he commented. He made his way over to the table, picked up and took a huge bite of a pulled pork sandwich that my wife had made for us.

"Muscles, when your wife is in her second trimester and riding your fucking dick all night, then we'll talk about sleeping when you're dead," Caleb grumbled, holstering his gun and crawling back into the recliner. His eyes once again closed and his arms crossed over his chest.

I chose to remain silent. Christi hadn't yet shown an increased interest in having sex. I was eagerly awaiting that particular side effect of pregnancy and was getting a bit irritated that shit hadn't kicked in yet.

"It can't be that bad. I mean what guy in their right mind turns down pussy?"

Books piped up at his question, "Muscles, does Ms. Ammo ever wake you up repeatedly during the night to fuck her?" His eyes closed again, his tone frustrated and very tired.

"Well, yeah, dude, when we were first married." Taking another huge bite of his sandwich, a small amount of sauce escaped and clung to his face. With a quick swipe of the back of his hand, he removed the red stain, and proceeded to drain his glass, washing it down. He then emitted a window shattering belch to announce his pleasure.

"No, motherfucker, I'm not talking about honeymoon sex. I'm talking about being woken from a sound-ass sleep to your wife riding your dick, not even giving you time to enjoy that shit." The raspiness and look of complete exhaustion told me that perhaps I should be glad Christi wasn't waking me to fuck my brains out.

"See, that's the difference between you and I, Caleb." Muscles never did know when to shut his mouth and leave well enough alone.

"Besides the obvious, please enlighten me." Caleb's voice was too calm, and I knew it was time to step in and defuse the situation. We had all been on edge since the warehouse break-ins. Today was intended to be relaxing and not worry about stupid shit.

"Books, how is Smiles? Nora said she had an ultrasound the other day." Da, the true patriarch of the family, beat me to it. Right after Christi and I announced our pregnancy, Smiles and Books announced they too were expecting. Christi joked about the house turning into a mini Toys-R-Us with all the babies that would be running around the house.

When Smiles confessed to Christi about being pregnant, she told her she already knew. After they left, I questioned her on what she meant and she told me that two of them had that 'twins' intuition thing. When they were growing up, they instantly knew when something had happened to the other, even if they weren't together.

"It was just a routine check-up. We had hoped to see what we're having, but the ultrasound technician said our baby wasn't cooperating. Everything is going fine otherwise." Books refused to get involved with anything that had to do with the day to day running of the family. He came in everyday, sat in his office, and took care of all the legal aspects of our business. He still carried a gun and was one hell of a fighter; he just preferred to keep us out of trouble with the IRS.

"Boss, if I wasn't already married to my Ammo, I'd marry your Christi," Muscles spoke around a mouthful of nachos. One thing was certain, that man could eat. Caleb had returned to his snoring and fuck-free sleeping, the prior argument as dead as he was to the world.

Since Christi became pregnant, she had been cooking like a mad woman; hell I didn't remember eating the same meal twice. She had jumped in headfirst with the decor and getting things ready for our baby. She came to me in a tear-filled confession that she felt awful that she had been neglecting me. As a result, the following week, she surprised me with the completion of this room.

When I first found this house, I pictured this room with imported rugs and stuffy furniture we would never sit on, but Christi had other plans. She had a company come in and build a television center to fit one of the solid walls, and then had surround sound in. She had a furniture maker come in and design a bar, with seating, so that no matter where you sat, you had a clear view of the game.

I was later told that Tonto helped her stock the bar and install a beer tap. She wanted me to have everything I would ever need when I wanted to escape. The day she led me by the hand into this room, I was so surprised I nearly squealed like a little girl . . . nearly.

"Boss . . . ?" I quickly turned my attention to Books. "I'm meeting with my college buddy this week."

Books had recently discovered that one of his college friends was currently working for the FBI. He had been out of the country for the past few months. I told Books to make the visit worth his time. If they were snooping around, I wanted inside information as to what they were looking for. It wouldn't be the first time an agent of theirs was able to retire from the department and start his own business. Our family was all too willing to pay for information that could be confirmed.

"Find out if there've been any changes in procedure," I instructed him.

"Yeah, and tell those fuckers they're going to get a bill for all the time I've spent away from my girl," Muscles added, disdain in his voice.

I was sick of the damage to my shipments. It had been months and we were no closer to knowing what was going on than when we started. I was at my wit's end with the waiting and staying up all night.

Tonto entered the room, a case of beer under his arm. He greeted each of the men with a one-armed hug and slap to the back.

"Boss, I love coming over to your house to watch the game. You always have a house full of very hot women."

I gave him a puzzled look as he placed his beer in the fridge behind the bar.

"You have all the ladies upstairs and a girl I've never seen before."

That got my attention.

I changed the channel on the television, bringing up the house security system. Before we had even moved into the house, I'd had cameras placed in every room. We would be having children soon and I wanted Christi to be able to have an extra set of eyes on our kids. I hadn't told her about the cameras yet. I wanted to surprise her when we brought our baby home.

The camera in the kitchen filled the screen with a color picture of our wives sitting around the bar. They were all laughing at something; it must have been good because Ammo had her hand over her mouth trying to keep the contents within contained The counters were covered in massive amounts of food, again with my wife's overzealous need for cooking these days. The mystery woman Tonto spoke of was none other than my new nuisance; Theresa Yancy. She had made it a point of being around Christi as much as possible. She would call at all hours of the day and night and show up almost as much. Unbeknownst to my wife, she also left not so subtle hints that she wouldn't mind 'getting to know me better.'

"Ugh . . . it's fucking Theresa." Her name came out as if I had swallowed a huge bug.

Da crossed the room and sat beside me, quietly questioning me with his face. "Not sure I like your tone, Son."

I tossed my head back and let out a long breath. I knew Da would not accept just a crass answer; he would want the entire story. I knew I would have to give him something.

"She first came over when we had our open house. Ma told Christi to invite the entire fucking block, and she did. Theresa was one of the neighbors who came, although she came with her husband. She's been over nearly every day since to visit with Christi. She's also made it abundantly clear that she'd like me to fuck her."

I rose from the couch and made my way to the bar for a new beer. I hated admitting this to my da, knowing what this ring represented in everyone eyes.

"I don't need to remind you of the consequences . . ."

I didn't let him finish.

"Da, even if I wasn't wearing this ring and I didn't take that oath with all of you, I still wouldn't do that to her, to . . . us."

The room was silent as da crossed the room to join me at the bar, his stance mirroring mine. He placed his arm around my shoulder and leaned into my side, speaking to me as a father and not the former leader of this family.

"I love you, Son, and I have high expectations that you'll honor your oath."

I placed my glass back on the bar, before turning in his direction.

"Da, my devotion to Christi has not one fucking thing to do with this ring." I raised my hand to emphasize my point, the ring in question on display, the heart in center glistening off the lights in the ceiling. She held my heart, from the first second I saw her, she had it.

"She's my entire world, without her smile in the morning, my day is shit. If something ever happened to her, you might as well shoot me in the fucking head because my life would be over."

Da did nothing to acknowledge my statement; I could see his words in his eyes. He shared the same devotion for my ma . He would not live long if she ever perished.

"So, this Theresa, what do we know about her other than she's a card carrying whore?"

I took a drink of my fresh beer before I set down the glass and turned again to face him.

"She's married, childless, and she lives in the house three doors over. She's trying to get a clothing line started. I can't remember the name . . ."

My da retrieved his phone from his pocket and sent a quick text to someone.

"Do you think you need to look deeper into her record, make

sure she checks out?"

I shook my head no. "I think it's just a harmless crush. I'm no stranger to crushes."

The Red Wings ended up winning, making Tonto a slightly richer man, cleaning house with the bet we'd had going. Everyone pitched in, helped clean up the dirty dishes and straighten up the place. Last thing any of us wanted was a pissed off wife.

I made my way into the kitchen and found my Christi sitting at the bar, a huge smile across her face. I wrapped my arms around her and attached my lips to her neck, causing her to squirm as my two-day-old scruff tickled her skin.

"Pa . . . trick!" She giggled as she said my name.

"Mmm," I sounded into her neck. I placed my hands over her perfect round stomach and my cheek to hers as I rocked her back and forth.

"How was your game, Babe?" She quietly questioned, her tone happy and content.

"Don't care; the food my fuck-hot girl made was the hit of the day." She turned her face toward me, her smile even bigger than when I first came into the room. "Thank you."

I pressed my lips to hers, turned her more toward me, and deepening the kiss. I made certain everyone in the room saw that kiss and my hands that continued to rub her belly. I had my own way of sending subtle messages that I was in no way interested in Theresa.

"I hear you two are having an ultrasound this week?" Ammo asked.

I didn't stop kissing my Christi's face as I answered her. "Yes, we'll see if the baby cooperates this time."

We'd had an ultrasound when Christi was twenty weeks, but our baby was stubborn and refused to spread those little legs. It seemed like the twin thing was continuing with their babes as well. Christi's doctor offered us a second opportunity to see the sex of the baby.

"Pfft! Doubtful; this is the child of you two, after all."

I didn't even try to comeback at that one since Ammo was correct; Christi and I both had a stubborn streak.

Monday morning found us heading to the doctor's office. Christi was sitting beside me as we drove down the street, hands intertwined, and soft music playing . I carefully pulled into a parking space, then made my way around to help my wife out of the car. Luck was on our side as the elevator doors were wide open as we approached. Keeping Christi's hand in mine, I placed her in the corner of the elevator and pressed the button for our floor.

The nurse took us back into the ultrasound room and gave Christi a gown to change into. Once she left the room, Christi removed her shirt and bra. Last night she must have hit her horny stage in the pregnancy as she woke me up three times to have sex. This morning, I woke to her riding me like a rodeo cowboy, her beautiful breasts bouncing in my line of vision. The girls had grown another cup size in the last few weeks. You could bet your ass I took those fuckers in my hands and mouth; making my girl scream.

Once Christi was dressed and sitting on the table, the tech knocked on the door and Christi told her to come in. Sandy was a middle-aged woman who wore her cat-eyed glasses on the end of her nose. She had short, bright red hair and red lipstick. She reminded me of a chubby Tammy Faye Baker.

"Good morning, Mr. and Mrs. Malloy. How are we today?"

Sandy took her seat and began to type on her keyboard.

"Very well, thank you," I replied.

"Are we ready to see what we're having?"

We both answered yes at the same time, laughing as I placed myself closer to my wife.

"Good, then let's get started."

Sandy lifted Christi's gown and applied some of the blue gel to her stomach. I asked Christi if it was cold, but she told me no, it was actually warm. Sandy informed us that all of her ultrasound gels sat on a heating pad, as using cold gel was just a mean thing to do to a pregnant lady, causing all of us to laugh. Sandy moved the wand around Christi's stomach for several minutes. The whoosh-whoosh sound of our baby's heartbeat filled the room and I couldn't help but smile.

"Dad, perhaps you should have a talk with your baby about co-operation."

I leaned my body over Christi's stomach and placed my index finger above her belly button.

"Hey, little one, can you cut your old man a break and do what Ms. Sandy wants you to do?"

Suddenly, the baby shifted on the screen and Sandy hit several buttons that froze the picture on the screen. She then took the mouse and pointed at what appeared to be the head of a turtle.

"Mom and Dad, I'm definitely a boy."

I looked at Christi to see her pointing at the monitor.

"Patrick, we're having a boy." Her voice was full of emotion, which triggered my emotions. I lowered my head and began to kiss her face, tasting the salt from the tears that were landing on her delicate face. I, Patrick Malloy, mob boss, was crying on my wife's face as I looked at the first pictures of my son.

Chapter Five

"**P**ATRICK, I WANT TO HOST an engagement party for Maggie and Angus."

I gave my Christi the look that, without question, said, "Are you asking or telling me? "

When Angus came to me and asked me for the use of my boat, I thought he would be using it that weekend or the next. However, he waited several months. I didn't, nor did I ever plan to, ask him why he'd waited. Listening to my Christi laugh and congratulate Maggie was my reward.

Her heart-stopping smile made my pulse increase as she cleared the distance between us. Her lips tasted of apple and spices and pure Christi. Her warm tongue carefully slid out to play with mine, and I moaned at the essence of it all. The tease let me only have a small sample before she withdrew and continued with what she was doing.

"I promise to keep it simple," she added, skimming the paper-work that now held her attention.

"Christi, you don't need my permission to spend money."

"I'm aware of this; I just like to keep you in the loop."

I tucked her closer as my hands drifted south to her hips. We were well into her pregnancy at this point. I had become very good at back and foot massages, as well as three o'clock in the morning supermarket and fast food drive-through runs. She continued to wake me at all hours of the day and night to take my cock in her mouth or her pussy, but I certainly did not complain.

"I thought we could have it here in the house, just close friends and family."

I nuzzled my face into her neck, nipping and kissing the entire area. I could feel her nipples harden as I continued my exploration of her body. I didn't wait for her to start things, I placed her on her side and began removing her pants. A small giggle escaped from her chest, but not a single word of objection was uttered. I kept her on her side as I entered her from behind; a position we both found worked well for us. I had access to all of her important triggers, and she could relax and get lost in my touch. My lips never left her neck as my hard cock slid gently into her wet folds. I loved my wife's swollen belly. She had been sexy as fuck when we first got married, but now she was absolutely irresistible. The softness of her skin and the delicate smell of her fragrance did nothing to discourage me.

"Patrick," she moaned, her voice laced with want, whisper soft. I knew what was coming, so I reached around, taking her erect nipple between my thumb and forefinger, adding slight pressure and a tugging motion.

"Shhh, baby, I've got you."

I moved my fingers from her nipple to her engorged clit, alternating between pinches and circles. Her body was shaking with her impending orgasm. The sensation giving me permission to let my own orgasm out of the gate.

"Mmm . . . Ooh," her voice was slightly high-pitched as her

shaking increased.

"That's a good girl, let it go, come all over my cock."

Suddenly, her hands were in the top of my hair as her orgasm hit her hard. I would swear to God she pulled out enough to make a bald spot, not that I uttered a single complaint. Her body jerked forward, reaching for that final rush of ecstasy.

"Oh, my God, Patrick!" Her breathing was ragged, her body moist with sweat.

"I know, sweet girl, I know." I pulled myself from around her and tossed my sleep pants on. Since the weather had become chilled, Christi had started drinking apple cider. I made it a point to have a hot cup of it waiting for her every morning.

As I descended the stairs, I heard the distinct sound of the shower running. Her cider would be the perfect temperature by the time she was finished. Making a cup for myself, I grabbed the newspaper and began reading to see if there was anything of interest.

Minutes later, a freshly showered and dressed Christi presented herself beside me. With an innocent kiss to my lips, she snuggled into. "Before I forget, Sherman and Sharon want us to attend a dinner party at their new house this Saturday." Christi removed herself from my arms and I offered her a steaming cup of hot cider. Sherman's vow to never get involved with another woman disappeared immediately after he laid eyes on Maggie's Ma, Sharon. She was a sweet, yet strong woman; nothing at all like Eileen. She took care of Sherman and made certain he knew how much he was loved.

I knew my wife well enough to know this was an event we would be attending. She might have been little, but she was full of hormones and could kill me if she chose to. In all honesty, she could get away with my murder because no judge in his right mind would convict a pregnant woman; again, the whole hormone issue.

"Let me know the time and I'll make certain I'm available to escort you."

"Sherman said five thirty; can you get away that early on Saturday?"

I kissed her forehead softly. "I'll talk to my boss; I'm certain she'll be fine with it."

She smiled at me as she smacked my bicep. "I love you," she chuckled as I left to go upstairs and get ready for the day.

Books had his meeting with his friend, Lucas, who told him no procedures had changed in regard to how evidence was handled. However, he did tell Books there was rumor of a particular agent who was in some trouble. He said he wasn't certain of the details, but he would do some digging. Books told him we would make it worth his time and gave him a sample of what this valuable information could bring him.

I had been riding Books hard to stay on Lucas to find out all he could about this agent in trouble. I had an eerie feeling about this situation. This could either work to our advantage or disadvantage, depending on what was happening. Since that first meeting, we hadn't had any more shipments broken into. My dad felt it was purely coincidental; I didn't agree.

I dressed in my new suit Christi had gotten me. I owned a million suits thanks to my sister, Amex, but this was the first one my wife had picked out for me, and I wore it with pride.

I made my way down the steps, only to stop short when I heard Theresa talking with Christi.

"So anyway, is Patrick going to be out again tonight?"

"I'm not sure."

"I don't know how you do it, Christi. I mean no offense, but your husband is pure sex on legs and I don't know if I could trust him to be out all night and not know what, or who, he was doing."

I wasn't going to let that bitch put thoughts like that in my girl's head, so I made a beeline for the kitchen. I didn't say a word as I snatched my wife up and kissed her with everything I had.

"You be ready when I get done with my meeting. I want to do something special with you tonight."

Christi didn't say a word; she only nodded her head and smiled the special smile she saved just for me. I kissed her nose, then dropped to my knees.

"Son, do me a favor and be extra nice to your ma. We're two lucky guys to have her and I plan on showing her every day for the rest of my life how much I love her."

I kissed her belly and headed toward the garage.

Take that, you nasty whore.

Saturday was a perfectly sunny day, totally abnormal for this time of year in Chicago. Sherman had sold everything he owned back in Mississippi and purchased a modest home here. Christi rang the doorbell and I wasn't surprised when Angus answered the door.

"Mrs. Christi," Angus greeted as he stepped aside, letting us pass.

"Angus, so good to see you. I hear congratulations are in order." Christi stood on her tiptoes and placed a gentle kiss on Angus's cheek. I watched the big man blush like an innocent virgin; I would tease him about it later.

"I'm just really lucky, is all," he responded honestly with a shrug.

Maggie was an amazing girl and she did right by Angus. They would be wonderful together; bringing the best out in each other.

"Good evening, Boss." The formality and respect was clear in his voice; he knew his place with me and respected my position.

"Angus."

Sherman and Sharon's house was what Christi referred to as 'classic Victorian.' Sharon had definitely done all of the decorating. It was tasteful and quite lavish. The tan walls and white trim allowed her to display her collection of antiques, which in my opinion were far too many. Christi kept our home simple and comfortable, not overly stuffed and unused.

The swaying of my beautiful wife's hips caused me to stop looking at the crystal chandelier and at her scrumptious ass. No matter how many times I had that woman in my bed, it would never be enough. If I had it my way, we would sneak off to one of the bathrooms and get in a quick fuck. The likelihood of that happening was slim as Christi wasn't that type of person; she would make me wait until we got home.

The sound of laughter, Muscles's laughter to be specific, sounded from the back of the house. I followed the swaying hips as the laughter became louder. Once we entered the kitchen, I found it to be standing room only as nearly thirty people were gathered around the oversized kitchen island. My ma sat on a high barstool with my father standing behind her, while Ammo and Smiles stood on either side of her.

"Boss, Mrs. Christi," someone spoke.

I watched as Ma's eyes lit up as she saw Christi walk toward her. Since we had gotten together, Ma had made it a point to take Christi under her wing, treating her as if she had been her daughter from birth. The situation benefited both woman and made my life easier.

I was surprised so many people were standing around. I honestly thought it would only be the four of us. I would ask Christi later if she'd known everyone would be here.

I looked around the room, but I couldn't find Sherman or Sharon, which I found to be very odd.

Food was laid out on the kitchen island and Muscles had made certain to taste test everything there. Christi quickly found the fruit tray and already began to enjoy the offerings there. Before I could ask why so many people were invited, Maggie appeared dressed in a beautiful teal evening gown and asked everyone to follow her. Taking Christi's hand in mine, we made our way in the direction Maggie was headed.

Sherman had built a sunroom after he purchased this house. Beyond that he had added a very large deck. He also had plans to add a swimming pool when the weather allowed. The sunroom was quite nice. Christi said she could just curl up in a chair and read for hours. Honestly, my wife could curl up in a bed of glass if she had a good book in her hand.

"Oh, my, Patrick! What do you suppose this means?"

The backyard had been transformed into a garden oasis. Directly in the middle was a white arch covered with yellow roses and teal ribbon. Lined in front of the arch were rows and rows of white chairs, teal ribbons adorning each one.

"Please take a seat and I'll let you in on our little surprise for tonight," Maggie's sweet voice directed, her angelic smile brighter than the sun.

As we all made our way to the chairs, my hand grasped in Christi's, I watched as Maggie stood in the middle of the arch.

"When I was a little girl living in Ireland, my ma always said there was someone for everyone. I never believed her, as I had watched too many people deliberately hurt one another. Nearly a year ago, I had the pleasure of meeting Christi Malloy. She inadvertently introduced me to my future husband. Thanks to her, I believe my mother."

I squeezed Christi's hand and she turned her attention to me, giving me her heart-racing smile in return.

"So today we have the honor of witnessing the union of two more hearts that have found one another; my mother, Sharon, and my soon-to-be father, Sherman Montgomery."

Harp music began to play as the French doors, which we had just moments ago walked through, slowly opened and Sherman's two Irish setters began to walk down the aisle. I had to chuckle as his male dog was dressed in a black bowtie and the female had a teal ribbon around her neck. My attention was again drawn to the front, where Sherman now stood under the arch. Caleb was standing with Angus beside him and the priest stood behind the lot.

The look on Sherman's face was of contentment and peace; exactly how I felt when I was with my Christi. Caleb's face was covered in a huge smile, and as I turned again, I found my sister walking down the aisle, her dress matching Maggie's. Maggie wasn't far behind her as soft gasps were murmured around the crowd.

When Sharon began to walk toward Sherman, it was as if no one else existed. Sherman was smiling so brightly I feared he would have cracks in his face.

Watching the pair as the priest read to them, I remembered how I felt when I stood in Sherman's shoes. Christi was right; everyone deserved to be loved and happy. I thanked God above that she chose me to love for the rest of our lives. I squeezed her hand, conveying silently that I loved her so very much.

When the ceremony was over, dinner was served and drinks flowed. Sherman made a toast to his new wife and explained to their guests that he and Sharon had agreed they didn't want anyone to feel the need to give a gift. They thought about going to Vegas, but Maggie told her ma she would never forgive her. So with the help of their children, they came up with this idea.

I held my wife tightly in my arms as I danced with her to the soft music that caressed us from the speakers around the yard. I smiled to myself and decided that life couldn't get much better than having my most treasured gift safely resting in my arms. The song was nearly over when my cell phone began to vibrate in my pocket. I didn't want to ruin the mood, but I knew Christi would get irritated if I didn't silence it. As I looked at my phone, I felt my anger begin to rise. The text was from Tonto.

Boss, security breach in the computer system. Shamus is working on it. Get here as soon as you can.

CHAPTER SIX

MY PARENTS INSISTED THAT CHRISTI go home with Ma. She kissed me soundly, promising me things she would gladly do to me if I hurried home. With a quick congratulations to Sherman and Sharon and a promise to have dinner later in the week, I waved goodbye to my wife. Once in the car, I phoned Matthew and had him head over to my parents' house. I didn't like where things were headed.

Da was sitting in the passenger seat, typing away on his phone, not a single word uttered by either of us. This security breach was just one more nail in my coffin. What kind of leader would I be if I couldn't protect myself and my family?

The trip downtown was a blur as I drove as fast as possible to the office. Da didn't even allow me to pull all the way into my parking spot before he dashed from the passenger seat. Inside the elevator, the only noise was the hum of the motor taking us to the top and the illumination of the lights as the floors passed. I felt sick to my stomach as I waited for the familiar tone of the floor being reached. This time I was the one to jump out first. I removed the tie and jacket I had worn to the wedding as I walked, then tossed the items inside the door of my office. I briskly made my way to the back of the condo where Shamus was waiting, his fingers flying across his keyboard.

Da was the first to speak as we came through the wooden door.

"Shamus, what do you have for us?"

His voice was even and devoid of emotion, his face, however, held fear and agitation.

"About an hour ago I was doing a routine clean up when I noticed something odd." Shamus's eyes never left the screen and his fingers never stopped typing.

Da moved around the desk and placed his hand on Shamus's shoulder, while pulling out his reading glasses, placing them on his face. "Define odd for me, Shamus," he instructed, his tone worried, yet calm. Even with the abundance of light in the room, the glare of the screen camouflaged Da's eyes from my view.

"Well, I started noticing little blips in certain files. The average IT person would've missed them because it acted as if the power went out and the battery backup came on. However, I did some research and found that no electrical outage was reported on those days. Furthermore, the last major storm was last spring."

I remembered that storm, but not for the same reason Shamus did. Christi and I had made good use of the lack of electricity, having had sex on every surface of this condo.

"I had to replace several batteries after that particular storm," Da added as he continued to face the screen, while Shamus typed away on his keyboard.

"I did a trace back to the IP address of the blips, and whoever did this knew what they were doing and how to hide it."

This got my attention. "Shamus, what did they take?"

Shamus stopped typing and turned his attention to me.

"That's the thing; the last three IP addresses were from public areas—the city library, a Starbucks, and the train station. They used the public WiFi as a cover, yet they took nothing; not one file was touched. I mean, if they'd wanted to they could've easily gotten into one of the bank accounts and drained it dry, but they didn't. It's as if they only wanted to have a quick look and then left."

Muscles was standing in the corner, his arms crossed and he was running his fingertips along his chin. "Shamus, do you think this is some basement hacker? Someone trying to impress his girlfriend?"

Da chuckled as he removed his glasses and moved slightly away, shaking his head as he lowered his gaze. How things had changed since he was the leader of this family.

"No, this is too advanced for computer geeks. My first thought was the Feds, but then I found the IP addresses and decided against it."

"Why?" I questioned.

"Well, they used public WiFi. The Feds have their own built into their computers," Shamus stated dismissively.

"True, but if they just needed a peek at something, maybe they had to use the public WiFi. As everyone knows, the government is cutting back on its spending," Caleb added. "Could it have been a case of the Feds being cheap bastards?"

Shamus began to run his hands through his hair. He was clearly puzzled. "It's not the Feds, guys! They have so many server protectors that keep out all public WiFi so their employees stay away from websites they shouldn't visit, such as porn," Shamus spoke from behind his hands that were still holding his face.

The room was silent as everyone absorbed this new information. Who would come in only to have a quick look around? What purpose would that serve?

"So, Shamus, what does all of this mean for us?" I questioned, my anxiety rising by the second.

Shamus sat back in his chair and looked me in the eye. "It means I'll be increasing the firewall and installing a new encrypting system; like the ones you see on the ticketmaster webpage where you have to unscramble the word to get access. Except for ours, it'll be a code that's unique to each of us; just in case this is someone on the inside."

I hadn't wanted to think of any of my men betraying me like that, but there it was.

"You said they only looked at certain files; do we know what files they looked into?" Da questioned. That particular thought had clearly eluded me.

"It'll take some time to follow the trail, but I've had a tracer on it since I discovered it."

Shamus began to type again as Books entered the room.

"I thought I heard voices."He looked surprised as he headed to the fax machine.

I looked at him questioningly. Could Books be the mole? If we even had a mole? This whole thing had me doubting my most trusted men. Books was family, yet, at this point, I needed to keep my eyes and ears open. I looked at Da, who appeared to have the same idea.

"Books, what are you doing here at this time?" Da questioned. The tone in his voice I had only experience a few time in my life. He, too, was questioning our men's loyalty.

"Remember, Boss? My sister is graduating from UCLA and I wanted to get all the bills paid before I left in a few weeks."

That was right; his sister was graduating with honors, a family trait I was told. He and Abby were flying out since Smiles was so close to her due date and the doctors refused to let her fly. She would be staying at our house.

"Oh, yeah, I did forget. Please give your sister our congratulations and have a great time."

"I will, Thomas, thank you."

I watched as the room began to empty. Shamus was lost in his computer, while my da was handing a white envelope to Books. I was about to head to my parents' house when my cell began to vibrate in my pocket.

I'm naked in our bed, baby is asleep, and I'm wet. Want to climb in and help me or should I start without you? ~C

I smiled as I pocketed my phone, grabbed my jacket and tie, and walked to the elevator, hitting the down button. I thought about texting her back and telling her I was on my way, but instead, I decided to just show up and surprise her. Maybe, just maybe, she would start without me; watching my Christi pleasure herself was a sight to see.

Two weeks later . . .

Tonight was Angus and Maggie's engagement party. I had strict instructions from my wife to be home and dressed no later than six o'clock. It was five-twenty and I was showered, shaved, and dressed.

Smiles had been staying with us for the past few days. I felt like Steve Martin in *Father of the Bride II* having two very pregnant women in the house. Honestly, I loved every minute of it.

Ma and Charlotte had taken over the engagement party planning. Christi gave orders and they made her suggestions happen. Everything was in place as my family had already started to arrive.

Muscles was posted at the door to make certain only invited guests were allowed in. At a little after six, the doorbell rang just as

I happened to walk by. I looked to Muscles and reached for the door. As I opened it, I had to fight my instincts to slam the door shut again. Standing on my front doorstep, dressed in a slutty, tight, red dress that barely hit mid-thigh, was the last person I wanted at this party: Theresa. She smiled with her glossy red lips and winked at me as she placed her fake fingernail between her teeth.

"Well, well, Patrick, don't you look yummy this evening."

My stomach turned at what she was implying. It was funny how having a beautiful woman by your side sours what would have sent me into an empty bathroom, with Theresa on her knees.

"What are you doing here? This is a private party." My clipped tone showing her how unwelcome she really was. I hated this woman.

"I know, silly. I was invited," she giggled as she spoke.

"Theresa, you made it," my wife's sweet voice came from behind me. She pressed past me and hugged her as if they were the best of friends. Something I hoped would fizzle out when she finally figured out I wasn't interested in anything but showing her the way out of my house and, by extension, my life.

"I wouldn't dream of missing this," Theresa answered her, but her eyes never left mine. I rapidly turned and left the two women together.

I found Smiles sitting in a chair in the editing room talking to Ammo and Amex.

"What's with the face, Patrick?" Smiles questioned, amusement in her voice.

"Oh, it's only that the bane of my existence just walked into my fucking house."

Smiles stood up and looked at the door. Christi was waving her arms around excitedly as she continued to speak with Theresa.

"Isn't that Theresa?"

"Uh huh."

"She isn't so bad, Patrick. She's been keeping Christi company."

I looked to Ammo who was still intently watching Christi and Theresa. Smiles had taken her seat again and began drinking her punch.

"Are you getting a bad feeling from her, Patrick?" Ammo turned to me and raised her brow in question.

"The only feeling I have for that woman is hate. She constantly makes it a point to let me know she'd like to take me for a test drive."

Ammo looked back to Theresa and Christi. "Need me to set her straight?"

Before I could answer her, Christi appeared beside me. "Hey, handsome, can I borrow you for a second?" She purred into my ear.

"For you, my love, anything."

Christi took me by my hand and led me to the kitchen. She found a corner where we could talk without being disturbed. She turned to face me and placed her hands on either side of my face. "Baby, I need you to do a favor for me."

I leaned down and placed a kiss to her perfect nose, nodding for her to continue. The girl had me by the balls since the first moment I laid eyes on her. The crazy girl had them displayed in a jar on the mantle.

"I need you to be nice to Theresa." I started to protest, but Christi quickly placed her index finger over my lips, silencing me. "I don't know why you don't like her and I don't care. She's been having a hard time lately and she needs a friend."

I reached up and removed her finger, gently kissing the tip.

"Patrick, she's trying to get her business off the ground and she's having trouble in her marriage."

She took her hand and cupped my face with it. I was lost in her big hazel eyes. Here stood the love of my life asking me to be nice to a woman she wrongly thought was her friend.

"Listen, she values my opinion and I'm trying to help her get her clothing line going." She took a deep breath and looked to my lips. "Patrick, she told me that her husband hasn't touched her in a very long time. She's convinced he's having an affair."

She closed her eyes and shook her head as if to shake off a bad memory. "I just can't imagine you ever doing that to me." Her voice a shiver of a whisper as she spoke.

I never wanted her to question my love and devotion to her. I leaned down and placed a kiss on her lips that said it all.

"Christi, I love you . . . if . . ."

"Christi!"

We both turned to the kitchen door to find a panicked Smiles standing over what appeared to be a puddle of water.

"Smiles?" Christi's panicked voice shrieked.

"Oh, my God! My water just broke! I can't have this baby yet . . . it's . . . it's too soon. I'm not due for another two weeks and . . . and . . . Dillion is in California."

I moved to Smiles's side. She reached out and grabbed my hand.

"Patrick, you have to get him back here, this baby can't be born without Dillion here."

I looked behind Smiles and noticed my parents were making their way over. Da was already talking on his cell phone.

"Smiles, honey, calm down. Remember, we sent Dillion on the family jet. I just spoke to the pilot who can have the plane ready and in the air in thirty minutes."

Smiles had her attention on Da, so I took the opportunity to get Books on the phone.

It rang three times before Books answered. "Yes, Boss, is there a problem?"

I chuckled as I answered him. "Not really, unless you consider you wife's water breaking in my kitchen a problem?"

"Oh, my God! Is she all right? Is the baby okay? Have you called an ambulance?" His rambling was so fast I nearly laughed . . . nearly.

"Books, you need to drop whatever you're doing and get back on the plane. It's waiting for you."

"Okay . . . um . . . I need . . . I need . . ."

"You need to get off this phone, grab Abby, and get to the airport. I'll make certain that someone is there to get you to the hospital."

I was pretty certain he completely dropped his phone and I could only pray he remembered to get Abby.

Twenty minutes later, we pulled into the hospital patient drop-off area. Ma, Christi, and Smiles were sitting in the back of Christi's SUV and Da was in the passenger seat beside me. He got out and smiled at the nurse and doctor who were waiting for us.

"I'll park the car and meet you guys in labor and delivery," I told Da.

"All right, Son, see you in a few."

I watched as Ma and Christi carefully helped Smiles out of the car. She wasn't in any noticeable pain, but she kept complaining that the water seemed to still be falling out of her. Ma only laughed at her and said just wait until that also happened when she laughed due to bladder problems. This caused Da and me to cringe and the girls to laugh at us.

After I parked the car, I received a text from the pilot that they were about to be in the air. He assured me both Books and Giggles were aboard. I found my parents sitting in the waiting room and joined them. Christi was in the room with Smiles and Matthew was on his way with Charlotte.

"I remember sitting in a room almost like this one when you were born," Da's voice broke the silence. "They told me to sit tight until they got her into bed and hooked up to monitors. I thought it was ridiculous as there wasn't an inch of your mother I wasn't acquainted with."

I physically shuddered at the thought of my parents in that way.

"My purpose in telling you this is that in a few short weeks, you'll be sitting right here . . . waiting. I just want you to take the time and practice being patient."

I had to agree with him; patience was not something I had been blessed with. Hell, I'd been known to yell at the fucking microwave.

"When it's Christi in there and it's my turn, I pray only for her to have an easy birthing experience. I don't like the thought of her in pain. I'll suffer in silence with my inability to be patient. I'll be there solely for her comfort."

Da smiled and patted my leg. "I knew I raised you right."

For the next few hours, we took turns going back and forth, checking to make certain Christi and Smiles had everything they needed. I finally received a text that the jet had landed safely and Muscles had them in the car.

I had just come from getting a second cup of coffee when the door of the elevator opened and a tired yet excited Books stepped into the hall. Abigail was nestled against his chest, her stuffed animal tucked in her arms.

"Please, tell me I'm not too late?" Books questioned in frantic exhaustion.

"No, she's been asking about you, though. Suite three, last one on the left," Christi spoke from behind me.

Ma came forward and gently took Abby from him. "Here, give

me my grandbaby."

A very sleepy Abby grumbled something that sounded like, "I'm a big sister."

I held my wife as we watched Books run down the hall. I moved her closer to my chest as both of my hands descended to her swollen womb that held my son. With a kiss to her neck, I led her over to the couch that rested against one wall. Three long hours later, Books made his way down the hall. His hair was a disheveled mess and his face was as bright as the sun.

"It's a boy! I have a son!" He shouted to the ceiling, his hands raised in victory.

Da was the first to jump to his feet and congratulate him. Abby was woken by Books's voice and removed herself from ma's lap and went to her da's side.

"Daddy, can I see my baby?" a very sleepy Abby questioned, her hand rubbing her left eye.

I watched as Christi's hand swiftly covered her lips, as a tear threatened to fall.

"Yes, my Princess, let's go see your new baby brother. Michael Patrick Dillion Parker."

CHAPTER SEVEN

IF THIS MORNING WAS ANY indication, today was going to be a bad day. I woke up late, spilled coffee on myself, twice, and then had a flat tire on my way to the office. As I sat in my meeting, I couldn't focus. Something bad was about to happen, I could feel it. We were still no closer to finding out who was trying to break into our computer systems and my nerves were pretty much shot.

The only bright spot was the memory of my beautiful Christi as she walked around our bedroom this morning. She had just entered her thirty-sixth week and also, it seemed, her nesting phase. I had come home two days ago to find her on her hands and knees, scrubbing the tile grout in the kitchen with a toothbrush. When I'd asked her what she was doing, she had told me she could not bring a baby into the house until it was clean. Ma reassured me it this was a normal stage of pregnancy and discouraged me from asking her to stop.

Today's meeting was to go over some information that one of the girls at the strip club had given us on some new punks trying to move into our neighborhood. They had been causing some trouble with the older residents. Da was old school and had no tolerance for that kind of behavior. Muscles was practically vibrating in his seat as he listened to the information.

Suddenly, the door flew open, causing the entire room's attention to shift. There stood my beautiful wife, angry and disheveled, her hair flying around her from the motion of the door flinging open. Her eyes were full of hate and disbelief, her chest heaving from her labored breathing. Her next words tipped my world onto an axis I feared we would never recover from and triggered events that put my life at risk.

Malloy residence, twenty minutes prior . . .

"Oh, my God! I can't believe how disgustingly dirty this house is!" Christi motioned around the perfectly clean house. Her arms flew up in exasperation and then slapped to the side of her thighs as she continued to look around.

"Christi, this house is not dirty.," Theresa corrected her with a laugh. "You're just nesting,." Theresa moved closer, intending to hug her friend.

"No, Theresa!" Christi stepped around her friends advances. "I can't bring Declan into this house with all of this dust and dirt. I mean if Child Protective Services were to take one look at my floors, they'd lock me away in jail." Her voice became high-pitched as she pointed to dirt that was invisible to the naked eye.

Theresa could only laugh at her as Christi continued to scrub the baseboards, wondering if the paint would survive the scrubbing it was subjected to.

"Well, I'm going to clean every inch of this house before my son comes home."

All week, Christi had been cleaning and re-cleaning the kitchen and family room. She had a company come out and clean out the air-conditioning ducts. Nora had refused to allow her to paint the nursery. She'd hired a professional painter, but he left a mess, so that was what she had cleaned yesterday.

Today, it was the master bedroom. Theresa had been an angel, helping Christi as much as she could. Christi felt so bad for taking up any of her time, since she was only days away from launching her line of women's clothing. Theresa had shown her several samples of some very risqué lace panties. Honestly, Christi thought some of her items were too . . . provocative for even a stripper to wear. She did, however, like her label . . . *Simply Theresa.* All of her undergarments had a dainty "ST" embroidered on them.

Christi walked into the closet and stood with her hands on her hips. All of Patrick's suits hung in color order and they would all need to go to the dry cleaners. No baby of hers would be held by a man wearing a dirty suit. She crossed the room and began removing the suits from their hangers. When she got to the dress shirts, she decided that they needed to be laundered as well.

"Christi, what on earth?"

Theresa stood in the doorway of the closet, hands on her hips, staring at the piles of suits and shirts that had been tossed out behind her in Christi's haste to clear them out of the closet. She rolled her eyes as Christi waddled back into the bedroom and began to pick up the jackets and go through the pockets.

Christi remembered how many times Patrick had left money or keys in his jacket pockets, so with a smile on her face she dug through the pocketed fabric with gusto. On top of the pile was the new Armani jacket she had recently purchased for Patrick. Memories of the last time she saw him wear it was to dinner at Sherman and Smiles's.

Christi looked up to Theresa's face as she reached into the inside pocket of the jacket. Theresa was looking at the jacket, her face reflecting memories that were playing inside of her own head, although the images were as different as day and night. Christi pushed her hand into the pocket and felt something soft and silky. She grabbed the item and slowly pulled it out.

She gasped as she looked at the item in her hand. Crumpled in the palm of her hand was a very slinky pair of Theresa's panties, the "ST" sitting right on top. Christi dropped the jacket and opened the panties. To her horror, she found a used condom rolled up inside of a Kleenex.

Patrick and Christi hadn't used condoms since the first couple of times they were together. Her body began to shake as it all hit her. Her eyes found Theresa's as the reality of her discovery began to set in.

"I'm so sorry, Christi," Theresa whispered, guilt coating her words.

Christi couldn't respond as the shock of it all crept into her bones.

"I told him we needed to tell you. I feel awful for deceiving you." Theresa's words seemed garbled to Christi's ears. She looked back to the condom and panties; noticing they had clearly been torn off of the wearer.

"Patrick said this was expected, that you'd have no problem turning a blind eye." Theresa's voice was pleading, whether it was for forgiveness or to justify her actions, it didn't matter, neither would be granted any time soon.

"Get out!" Christi ordered as she continued to look at the material in her hands. Her voice was even and monotone, calm if only for the moment.

"Christi, you had to suspect something. He was with me every night for months . . ."

"I said, get out!" The emotion and anger causing her volume to increase. Christi's eyes closed, she was trying desperately to keep her emotions in check.

"Patrick is a powerful man who has needs and, you know, you've been really large for quite a while now," Theresa continued. "So I'm sure it was difficult for him to be intimate with you. Did you really think he was working all those nights?"

It was in that moment that she lost her battle to remain calm. Anger and absolute mortification had built like a pressure cooker inside of her until it boiled over. She was now powerless to do anything about it except release the valve and let out the pain.

"I said, get the fuck out!" The final word shouted and revealing the power of Christi's temper.

This time her eyes grew large and she turned rapidly. Christi watched as Theresa ran down the stairs and out the front door, slamming the wooden door causing the glass to vibrate.

How could he? How could he lie to her face for months?

Christi didn't remember the ride to Patrick's office, but here she was, sitting in the SUV he had bought her and wearing the maternity clothes he had surprised her with. Still clasped in her hand were the nasty panties of the whore he had fucked behind her back, possibly in their home.

She entered the condo where no one was standing guard; like that mattered to her. In her current state, she dared anyone to try and stop her. She could hear Thomas's voice as she walked down the hall. She threw open the double doors, anticipating having at least one gun pointed at her, but there were none that she noticed. As she made her way around the large table, Thomas called her name, but she ignored him.

"Out!" Christi shouted into the room, her eyes landing on a shocked Patrick.

"Babe?" Patrick questioned.

"I fucking said everyone get the fuck out!"

"Christi? Honey . . . ?"

"If you don't want everyone hearing this, you'd better order them out . . . now!"

She watched as Patrick stood from his chair, slowly reaching out his hand to her.

"Christi, honey, calm . . ."

"Fuck you!" She shouted and then slapped his face. She watched as his head snapped to the side and she had the desire to do it again. She wanted to slap him repeatedly over and over until he felt as bad as she did. But she would never be able to hit him hard enough to quiet the rage she had inside her. Turning her attention to the men in the room, she spoke the words that begged to come out.

"I bet all of you knew about this, didn't you? You sorry, motherfuckers! Were you laughing behind my back? High-fiving him each time he did it?"

"Christi, sweet . . ."

"No, Thomas, I wouldn't believe you, either!" Her hand was raised in the air, her palm facing him, giving no room to continue. "You're most likely doing the same fucking thing to Nora. Is she expected to turn her back, too? Allow you to have a little side action when things get rough or boring at home?"

"Christi, seriously, can you please calm down?"

"No, Patrick, I won't calm down!" She slammed the panties and condom on the table for all to see. "I found these in your jacket, the one I bought for you. The one you wore while you fucked your whore."

"Babe . . ."

"No! I told you from the very beginning," she slapped her hand on the table after every word, stinging her palm, but she didn't care. "I told you that I refused to turn a blind eye to you having a fucking *mot* on the side!"

Patrick didn't respond this time; he and Thomas both remained silent. Both dazed and confused, completely lost as to what she was shouting about.

"You swore to me, over and over, that you couldn't do that. You said you didn't have it in you."

"Christi, I can see why you'd be upset," Thomas started in a calm voice. He was trying to calm her down, knowing stress wasn't good for her or the baby.

"Oh, no! I passed upset when Theresa told me she and Patrick had been fucking behind my back for months. Months, Patrick! You fucked her for months!" She shouted as she again pounded the table, enunciating every word.

"Christi?" Caleb questioned, attempting to be calming, but to Christi it was futile.

She refused to listen; all of his men would stand behind him. She left the room and as she entered the hallway, she clearly heard Thomas tell Patrick, "Let her go, Son." These words only confirmed for her heart, what her mind already suspected was completely true.

Christi had never been so grateful for kind people as she was when she entered her OB/GYN's office. She informed the reception-ist that she had an urgent personal matter to discuss with her doctor. The nurse, taking one look at her appearance, motioned for her to come on back. Once she was seated on the exam table, the doctor came in. For the next thirty minutes, she cried as explained what she had recently discovered and shared her current fear that she was walking around with some life threatening STD. Her doctor agreed and ordered some blood work, requesting the results as soon as possible.

As Christi lay on the crinkling paper, humiliation and despair set in. She had gone against her basic instincts when it came to Patrick; ignored the voice that had screamed at her she wasn't the type of woman he needed. Now she would have to live with the decision she'd made, against her better judgment. With her knees in the air and her pride no longer a character flaw, she vowed she would never again ignore that tiny voice ever.

Once she was back in the car, she remembered Shane McIntyre was Patrick's lawyer. She knew it would be a conflict of interest to ask him to represent her, but maybe he had the name of someone she could use.

When she called McIntyre's office, she didn't disclose to him what she needed an attorney for and he didn't question her. He informed her that his daughter was trying to build up her clientele up, that she was sharp as a tack, and tough as nails. He gave her the number and Christi called her immediately. Ms. McIntyre agreed to meet with her. Once again, she told the twisted tale of betrayal by her husband and supposed best friend.

"Well, Christi, I have good news and bad news," Ms. McIntyre said from across her desk.

"Trust me, your bad news will never compare to mine."

"Well, Illinois law prohibits pregnant women from petitioning the courts for a divorce."

Gretchen McIntyre was a red-haired beauty. Her shoot from the hip attitude gave Christi the sense that she could trust her, even after informing her who Patrick Malloy was and what his business entailed. Gretchen voiced that she couldn't wait for the challenge.

"They feel you aren't in control of your emotions. The good news, however, is that I can get the paperwork together and I can have it filed the moment you give birth."

Gretchen asked several more questions about Patrick's infidelity. Then she asked Christi a question Christi hadn't really thought about.

"What demands do you have for compensation? Child support? Alimony?"

With fire in her eyes and a pat to her swollen belly, she replied with conviction and determination. "The only thing I want is my name back and him out of my life."

Gretchen extended her hand and a deal was struck. Patrick would receive the divorce petition the second Declan was born. Christi offered to pay extra if Gretchen would serve them while he was shacking up with his new whore.

By the time she arrived back at home, it was well after dark. She was so tired, both emotionally and physically, that she parked the car in the driveway and made her way into the house. Everything was just as it was when she had left; it didn't appear that Patrick had been by. She suspected where he was, but chose to push those thoughts from her mind. She looked at the couch that sat facing the fireplace. She questioned if he had ever fucked Theresa in this house; on that couch or on the floor where they had made love so many times.

She couldn't take it anymore. The memories mixed in with the betrayal, she had enough. She pushed it all away, turned to go out the door, and got back into her car. She drove around until morning, trying to put enough space between herself and all the pain that chased her. When she could barely keep her eyes open, she found a hotel that she felt was safe. As she got out of the car, she noticed a maternity shop across the street. She made her way into the shop, where she purchased new clothes with her own personal credit card; the one she had from before they were married. She ducked into the dressing room and stripped out of the clothes that Patrick had purchased and tossed them into the trash before redressing. She wanted nothing from the man who had betrayed her in the worst way.

She checked into the hotel, using her maiden name, and the credit card that she had used across the street. The man behind the counter never questioned why she was checking in so early in the morning. When she finally lay down, exhausted, on the hotel bed, she felt the first tear fall down her face. She placed her hand on her stomach, vowing that she wouldn't let this break her. She would raise Declan by herself. She didn't need Patrick or his money. Her father had done just fine raising three girls by himself. A single baby would be a piece of cake.

She allowed the tears to take over, purging her sadness and embarrassment. She would allow herself this just once. Tomorrow, the day after, and every day after that, she would get up, dust herself off, and live for the little miracle that was kicking within her belly. This would be a lesson; a lesson she would learn the first time. Patrick Malloy might have fooled her, but he didn't break her. At some point, in her self-declaration she managed to drift off, but suddenly woke with a start, a sharp pain in her lower back. She sat up in bed, only to come to the realization that her water had broken.

Only one thought made its way through her lips. "Oh, God, no, not today."

CHAPTER EIGHT

THIS HAD TO BE A dream. I was certain I would wake up any minute and I would be back in my bed, wrapped around my wife. I would tease her about her excessive cleaning and she would smack me, telling me to shut up. She would walk around, her belly swollen with little Declan safely growing inside her. Except, when I opened my eyes, the sad and confused eyes that looked back at me dashed any hope I had of this being just some head trip induced by too much whiskey.

No one was speaking or moving. I lowered my eyes back to the grainy lines of the table. the same table where Christi had slammed her hand repeatedly as she accused me of defiling our marriage. My stomach turned at the vile notion that such a thing could even enter her mind. I had never given her the slightest reason to believe I had done anything to ruin us.

"Patrick, I have to ask . . . ?" Da's voice shattered the silence, causing reality to come crashing down. I knew the question before it left his mouth.

"If you have to ask, then you might as well kill me right fucking now!" I seethed. "I don't need a goddamn ring to remind me what's important in my world." The very ring now sat cold and dead against the skin of my finger, just like my heart, the life it once held was fleeting.

The lace scraps still sat on the table, a glimpse of a yellow condom peaked out of the tissue. How could little lies come in such pretty wrapping? Its secrets on display for anyone who dared to look. Sadly, that observer was my wife.

"So, tell me what you know about this Theresa person who has lied to our Christi." Sherman spoke from behind me. His non cavalier attitude was refreshing, giving me something to focus on. It kept me from jumping out of my skin and filling the room with all of the rage I felt. Although, it begged, like an anxious dog, to be let out.

"She's one of our neighbors. She lives a few houses down from us with her husband, Clark, but I've only seen him once at our open house. Geeky motherfucker, dressed like his mother laid out his clothes or something. Said he sold insurance, but didn't try to get a single digit the whole night. Christi said he works crazy hours and Theresa thought he was having an affair."

"What's the last name?" Shamus asked.

"Johnson."

"Couldn't get anymore generic if he invented the fucking thing." Shamus's fingers stilled for just a second and then went back to warp speed across the keys. The pause between the last two words died as soon as it left his mouth.

I needed to get out of this room. I needed to go after Christi, beg her to listen to me. Either that or beat the shit out of something or someone.

"Shamus, have all of Patrick and Christi's credit cards monitored. I want to know about any charges she tries to make." Da was typing away on his phone, his glasses still resting on his nose as he gave the order.

"Da?"

"Patrick, she is clearly upset. She is also very pregnant and I doubt she'll return to the house where she believes you had a mistress."

Fuck, he was right. The house we had made a home was now a painful memory for her. I had to fix that. Hell, I'd buy her a new one if she wanted; anything just to bring her back to me.

"What about her cell phone? Can we trace it?" I added.

"Sorry, Boss, already thought of that," Shamus responded. "She turned it off and removed the tracking card."

"What about her car?"

Shamus could only sigh. "It runs off her cell phone."

"What about her shamrock? We give them that fucking thing for a reason." My voice was angry and frustrated. All the extra security we had put in place since her kidnapping and it was all shit.

"That appears to be located at an address you know well . . . her OB/GYN's office. I tried calling to see if anyone found her necklace and they said she left it behind, but they've not been able to reach her." Shamus had a look on his face, a look I knew held more information, news I didn't want to hear.

"Tell me, Shamus!" I commanded.

"She *uh* . . ." His head bowed, the typing had ended and his hands were now on the back of his neck. His eyes landed on everything but my face. "She took you off all her paperwork. You can't get any information about her from her doctor."

I'd been in my fair share of fights, punched by some pretty big motherfuckers, not a single one of them hurt as much as what hearing that shit did. On her first visit I gave her so much shit about spelling my name correctly, she leaned over and kissed my nose, telling me that she stole my last name fair and square and wasn't giving it back. Yet, in the blink of an eye, one single event threatens to change everything we'd built. So, with all my resources, power, and money, I sat here, with no idea where my wife was, knowing she believed a lie.

"I have to get out of here. I have to see if I can find her."

I didn't let anyone try and stop me. I ran down the hall and into the elevator; Christi's perfume still lingered there. My chest felt tight and it took everything I had not to crumble down onto the floor and cry. Instead, I pounded my fist as hard as I could into the metal of the wall of the elevator. The burn of my actions did nothing to relieve the ache in my chest and the fear that had bubbled in my throat.

The first place I looked was Coleen's grave. She had a habit of going there when something was bothering her, but the headstone was vacant. Next, I headed to Books's house. Her sister had just had the baby and I knew she would be home. Smiles answered the door with little Michael snuggled in her arms. My chest ache deepened as I watched him sleep safely in his mother's embrace.

"Patrick, this is a surprise!" Always a smile on her face, ever since meeting Books and getting married. They complemented each other. I remembered when Books first came to me with the idea of asking Smiles out. He knew of my intentions with Christi; he was the one who had alerted me about Douce fighting in the lobby and how Christi was breaking it up. I pussied out that night. I had every intention of asking her out, but then the bomb was dropped about Giggles and my plans changed. Da had to keep me from killing Douce when I found out what he was up to; instead I broke his fucking jaw and three ribs.

"I'm sorry to come over unannounced, but have you seen Christi today?"

"No, she and I haven't spoken since last night. Theresa was going over to your house and helping her with some project she has."

Smiles began to rock her body back and forth as little Michael began to fuss.

"What happened Patrick?" Her face had concern written all over it.

I hung my head as she invited me in. I sat on her couch and told her everything that had happened in my office. I nearly lost it again when I told her about how Christi had walked out.

"Well, I have to say that I never got a good feeling about Theresa. She was just too, I don't know, full of herself." Smiles tossed her free hand around in the air, her red hair bouncing with her movement. This was interesting. Christi had never mentioned she and her sister had disagreed about Theresa. "As far as Christi is concerned, you know she won't do anything foolish to hurt herself or the baby. But you and I both know that when she gets mad . . ." Her voice became amused, Christi was very headstrong when she was passionate about something. I knew very well how Christi acted when she was angry. The incident with Anthony and the flowers came to mind. "I wish I could tell you that she'll cool off and come looking for you, but I can't." Her hand touched my arm and I knew Smiles was right, Christi wasn't in control of her emotions right now. I needed to find her before she let them get the best of her. Knowing she had visited her physician was also tugging at the back of my mind. "If I see or hear from her, I will let you know," she assured me, placing her hand on my cheek. I thanked her and made my way to the door, but her voice called me back. "Patrick, swear to me you didn't do what Theresa accused you of." I turned and looked directly into Smiles's eyes. "I swear on my life." Smiles would never know how true a statement that really was.

For the next ten hours, I drove to every place in Chicago I could think of. I went to her favorite places and even spoke to several people in her old neighborhood—nothing. It was as if she had vanished.

Finally, I decided I couldn't keep my focus anymore and headed to my parents' home. I couldn't bear the thought of being in my house without my wife. The house was alive, if the amount of lights on and the number of cars that were parked in the driveway were any indication.

I entered the front door and headed straight for the kitchen, ignoring the guards who greeted me and closed the door. I knew beyond a shadow of a doubt that my ma would be there. As I rounded the corner, there she stood, her face sad and drawn. She loved Christi, maybe more than she loved me, I honestly believed. I collapsed to my knees, buried my face in her shirt, and wrapped my arms around her, securing myself to her. She would never judge me or expect me to maintain my image, the one created by the power and guns I held. She was my ma; she loved me without question and gave comfort without being asked. "She's gone, Ma"

"I know, Son, but we will get her back." Her voice was soft, her fingers combing through my hair, just like Christi did when I snuggled into her side. "How?" I cried into her shirt. "Because, I believe in the truth. That, and all the information your men found while you were out scouring the city." I immediately pulled my head back and looked up at her. Her face contained just a hint of a smile, enough that I was able to stand and comb my hair back with my fingers. "Son, come into the den and we'll talk," Da said behind me.

I stood, walked over to the sink, and ran cold water over my face.

Ma handed me a towel and then kissed me on the cheek. Nearly my entire inner circle was in the room, all with the same expression and goal. My father handed me a cup of coffee and it was then I noticed the sun was coming up. Christi had been out there all night, by herself, unprotected. I prayed to God she was safe. "So, what have we got?" I spoke to everyone in the room.

Shamus spoke first. "Well, I checked out the name you gave me, Theresa Johnson, and found that a twenty-two-year-old, white female of the same name, residing in Ashton, Arkansas, was killed last year in a head on collision. The article I found stated she was on her way to catch a plane to New York to meet a buyer from Saks Fifth Avenue, to carry her line of women's underwear." Shamus looked up and met my eyes. The expression I gave him didn't need to be voiced, *keep talking motherfucker.*

"Since, I knew there had to be more, I kept digging. I mean, if you have clothes to sell to someone like Saks, then you have to have storage somewhere." He was right; I wouldn't have thought about it. "Seems that Mrs.Johnson was also in the car when it crashed and was in the hospital for a few weeks. After several months in rehab, learning to walk again, she came home to find that no one had been paying on the storage facility where Theresa kept her clothing. I contacted the storage facility and it seems they had one of those auctions like you see on reality television. A couple by the last name of Stone runs the auction. I looked into their records and found out who purchased the storage shed in question. Records show a female by the name of, Rebecca Young, purchased the contents of the storage container. I had to really dig deep into Ms. Young's background, but what I found was quite interesting." Shamus slid out a file from beside him in the chair. Da handed it to me as Shamus continued. "It seems that Rebecca has quite a rap sheet; longer than Muscles, actually." I knew it was meant to be funny, but I had no ability to laugh. "She's been charged several times with credit card fraud and petty theft. Nothing that would make me suspicious." Shamus pulled out another folder and, again, handed it to Da. He took a quick look and passed it to me. I opened it and was astonished at what I found.

"I checked the county registrar's office to see if Rebecca owned any property and found that she doesn't have any property. Her driver's license also expired a few years ago. What I did find, however, and you can clearly see for yourself, the house that Theresa claims to live in, has been vacant for three years. The last legal owners walked away from it when the husband died. I then went to the house myself and checked, Boss, the house is completely empty." I couldn't believe my eyes as I continued to look at the pages in front of me. Theresa had lied about everything.

"I figured Theresa had to live somewhere, so I had Tonto stake out your house to see if she tried to return. He didn't have to wait long until she did and knocked at your front door just after six last night. She walked around as though she was trying to find a way in, but left empty-handed. Tonto followed her downtown where she stopped at a drug store and purchased a home pregnancy test. He followed her to what we found out to be her real address."

"Rebecca Young, aka Theresa Johnson, aka Melanie Storm, aka too many fucking names to continue, lives above the Starbucks that one of the pings to the computer system originated from." My eyes went directly to Tonto's. "Are you sure she lives there?"

"Yes, Boss. I paid her landlord three hundred bucks to confirm it, even showed him a picture that Shamus gave me. He said he was sure it was the lady he rents to." I looked back to Shamus. "Is that all?" Shamus shook his head and leaned his forearms on his knees. "Not by a long shot, Boss." Caleb stood up this time and made his way to my father's desk that sat in the corner. He flipped open the laptop that sat on there as he began to speak. "When my father and I found out what Shamus and Tonto had discovered, I had Shamus do a little further investigating. Dad took the condom and panties and sent them to a friend of ours who owed us a favor." I looked to Ma, who now stood behind my father, her eyes welling with tears.

"Dad suggested that since Theresa was milling around the house, she must have left something behind. He had Shamus pull up the security tapes for the last few days. Unfortunately, we found nothing unusual . . . at first." Caleb pushed a few buttons on the laptop and the flat screen on the wall came to life. There on the screen was my closet. I noticed nothing out of the ordinary. "I don't see what you're trying to show me."

"We didn't notice anything either. Then, I thought, what if Theresa planted those panties in your closet? I knew you had cameras all over the place, so I had Shamus go back three weeks."

I, again, looked at the same screen, nothing.

"Okay, so what did we see?"

"That's the thing, Boss, we saw three weeks of this, nothing. Not one piece of clothing moved, not one person entered or left the closet."

That got my attention. There was an evening, not even a week ago, when I was getting ready for a meeting, Christi had come into that very closet and begun to stroke my cock. She then bent over, leaning on the center cabinet while I pounded into her, as she begged me to fuck her hard. I was late to the meeting; but that wasn't the only thing I remembered.

"Go back to the night of Sherman's wedding," I instructed.Caleb moved the timeline to the appropriate spot. "Well, fuck me running." Everyone looked at me and then to the screen. "Christi bought me a new suit. I hung it on the valet stand that's right there in the room."

The mahogany valet stand was completely empty.

"Just wait, Boss, there's more."

I looked at Caleb, who was again pressing keys. "When Christi told Nora she was expecting, she went out and bought a monitor for the baby's room. That monitor has its own recording system." The screen changed to Declan's nursery and I watched as frame after frame went by. I nearly lost my breath when suddenly I saw Theresa standing in the doorway, holding the panties and what looked to be the used condom in her hand. She casually walked over to the crib and ran her fingers up and down the railing. She then looked at her watch and made her way back toward the door. She looked in both directions and then walked to the right, straight for our bedroom.

Shamus's phone began to ring as Caleb turned off the flat screen. I couldn't look at it anymore. I had to find Christi, show her what we found. She would have to come back to me then.

"Boss, that was my friend at NCIS crime lab."

Before Shamus could continue, my father's phone began to ring.I looked to Shamus as my father left the room to take the call. "That was Books." Sherman looked back at Caleb, as he continued. "His friend at the FBI just called him." My father chose that moment to come back into the room. "Nora, I need to see you out in the hall, please."

I watched as Ma left the room. The hairs on the back of my neck stood straight up. Da had never asked Ma to leave the room before. I didn't like the feeling I was getting. Something was wrong, very fucking wrong. I looked back at Sherman, whose eyes were still fixed on mine.

"They've made an arrest within the department."

I could hear ma crying in the hall. A sixth sense told me something had happened to Christi. I rose from the chair and began to make my way out to the hall. I opened the door and watched as Ma closed the front door.

"What the hell is going on, Da?" My father was just finishing up a phone call. I clearly heard him say, "Take care of it McIntyre!" The look on his face was of defeat and sadness. He took in a deep breath before he raised his eyes to mine.

"Patrick . . ."

Matthew now stood inside the door where ma had just exited. His face was ashen and somber. "Matthew, by the look on your face, I know you've heard." Matthew only nodded and looked to the floor. "Yes, Christi called me, she told me a few things. Mostly, a message to give to you." I watched as his sad eyes shifted from my face, to Da, and back.

"She's in labor. She says you can come to see your child being born, but . . ."

My heart began to race, Declan wasn't due for a few weeks, could this be the reason she went to see her doctor today? Had the stress of all of this caused harm to my son? Matthew put his fingers up for quotations, " . . . but 'he better keep his whore at home'."

CHAPTER NINE

C HRISTI WAS HAVING MY BABY, the thought playing over and over inside my head. This whole fucked up situation with Theresa would have to wait. I needed to be there for the both of them. "Matthew, I'll follow you to the hospital." My keys were already in my hand, my mind on the quickest way to get there. "Actually, I'd like to ride with you; tell you what I know about what has happened." I nodded my head and motioned for him to go ahead out the door. I turned back to my family, who remained behind me, looked straight into Sherman's eyes and barked out my instructions. "You find that fucking cunt and you bring her here! I'll deal with her once I get my family back."

The hospital Christi and I had chosen was only fifteen minutes away. She'd even had me do several test runs to be sure I could get there on time. I'd always assumed she would be in the car beside me when it was time.

"She stayed in a hotel until her water broke a few hours ago." Matthew's voice sounding angry and tired—I could understand both. "Tells me she has proof you stepped out on her. Fucked some girl she's friends with." I closed my eyes briefly and took a deep breath. My explanation was on the tip of my tongue, but was cut off as he continued.

"I was there when you took that oath, gave your word to every man who listened. I gave you my trust. I went to bat for you when she had convinced herself she wasn't good enough for you. That she couldn't be the type of woman you needed her to be. She said she would never turn a blind eye to what you did and I swore to her she wouldn't have to." He paused for a moment, the emotion in his voice caused me to choke up. "Your father won't have to be the man to kill you." His voice was now full of hatred. "I'll kill you myself!"

The car was silent as I let him have his moment. I tried to place myself in his shoes, giving my daughter to a man with my character. Knowing me as I did, we would have never made it to the inside of this car.I would have killed the bastard for hurting my baby girl. When there were only a few minutes before we arrived at the hospital, I filled him in on everything we had learned. He sat in silence, eyes cast out the window, as the buildings of downtown Chicago continued to flash by.

"She isn't going to listen." He shook his head. "She has her mind fixed on being angry with you. She's going to yell and scream at you, call you everything but a good man."

I didn't even look at him as I pulled into the parking garage, sliding fluidly into a parking spot. "Nothing worth having is easy, didn't you tell me that?" I pulled my keys from the ignition and tossed my sunglasses in the center console. "She has every right to be angry; her friend just betrayed her by making her think the man she gave her heart and soul to tossed it away. But, at the end of the day, I *will* get her back."

I hated hospitals. The sounds and smells reminded me too much of the days I spent at Christi's bedside after the kidnapping—making bargain after bargain for her to return to me. Now, I had a new deal to make, a wrong to be righted. I confidently followed Matthew to the room that held my entire world. Christi was, above all, an intelligent woman who was rational and a believer in the truth. Once all the evidence was presented to her, she would feel crazy for doubting me and we could go back to being a solid unit.

Matthew knocked on the closed door, opening it slightly and poking his head in"Sweetheart?" His voice sweet and pleading, causing my nerves to return. "Did you find him?" Her tone was all wrong, clipped and full of hatred. "Was he fucking that whore of his?" Matthew glanced back in my direction, his eyes apologetic, before opening the door wide for me. Ma stood beside my wife's bed, a plastic spoon in her hand with what appeared to be ice chips, her face covered in fear. "You!" She shouted, pointing a finger in my direction, her IV tubing dangling from her wrist. "Can stay in that corner and shut the fuck up!" Christi looked tired. Her hair that once bounced and shined, was now flat and stuck to her head. Her eyes that once danced with excitement, held nothing but pain and resentment. There was a puffy area that marred her perfect skin under her eyes. She was still beautiful, still the girl I was madly in love with.

"You don't get to say anything, not a single word."

I nodded my head and took a seat in the corner she indicated. I would do as she asked; give her a little time to cool off before I attempted to reason with her. Before I showed her the evidence we had against the bullshit Theresa had spewed.

Sitting in the cold, plastic chair—a tiny prison cell my wife had placed me in—I took a look about the room. Christi was reclining and appeared comfortable for the moment. Ma was now talking to her in hushed tones, telling her story after story to rid her mind of not only the pain she was trying and failing to hide, but the dire situation we found ourselves in. A heartbeat thumped in quick time, filling the room. My son's heartbeat to be exact. I held on to that sound, the swishing of the movement as he tried to make his way into this world. His imminent appearance made all of this seem so small, so petty. When this was over and the truth was finally heard, I was going to make certain no one could damage my family like this ever again.

The tension in the room was so thick you could almost see it. Christi's doctor came in and checked her progression. I tried to sit quietly and give her the space she needed. She was angry enough that she could have me thrown out of this room, preventing me from watching Declan's birth. I would sit here like she asked me to or get her anything she needed, and when this was all over, I would take my family home.

"Do you have any idea how embarrassing it is to have to admit that you have reason to believe you've been exposed to harmful diseases?"

I looked to ma, who was reading a magazine quietly in her chair. She shook her head, letting me know to remain quiet.

"To have to buy new clothes because you're ashamed of the ones you walked into the store with? To check into a hotel because your home isn't your home anymore?" It was slight, but her voice cracked as she confessed how she spent the past day away from me. "Intentionally leaving a piece of jewelry in the trash because you can't stand the lie it represents?"

I had reached my limit, listening to her voice crumble and watching the exhaustion setting into her tiny body. Just when I was about to end this, she cried out and grabbed her stomach. Ma was right beside her, encouraging her and telling her that everything was all right. Matthew had left the room, deciding his job was to remain in the waiting area, far away from the battle zone in this room.

"Christi, you need to breathe, Lass." Ma took her hand between the both of hers. "Being this stressed and upset won't get this baby born any faster." Christi continued to writhe in pain. It was beyond my ability to witness and do nothing about, so I bolted out of the room and got the attention of one of the nurses in the hall.

Christ was still tossing back and forth from more pain than I thought she could ever manage. The nurse entered confidently and grabbed a pair of gloves from a drawer, pulled up the sheet that covered the lower half of my wife, and began to examine her. With one hand gripping Christi's raised leg, her face made conflicting expressions, and then she withdrew her hand, replacing the sheet.

"Well, Mrs. Malloy, it's time to give that little one a birthday."

A flurry of activity began the second the nurse left the room. First, Christi's bed was converted into a chair that looked like it belonged in a dentist's office, instead of a hospital room. The nurse who checked her a second ago, returned with a team of people. They pushed a large cart that had a plethora of tools and equipment wrapped in blue paper on it. Christi's doctor came in wearing a drape over her clothing and plastic glasses on her face. Another nurse brought in what looked to be a space aged crib; it had light at the top and monitors on the sides. I was in awe at how they worked so fluidly together. Christi's doctor was now sitting in a chair between her legs. Christi was draped in the same blue material that covered the tools on the tray and a nurse was insisting I put on the same drape everyone else was wearing.

"Patrick!" Christi cried. I didn't hesitate to cross the room and stand by her side. She reached out and grabbed my hand, squeezing the blood right out of my fingers. It was then, as I was so close I noticed she no longer had her wedding rings on. I hoped it was just because of where she was and not because she was finished with our marriage.

"You can . . ." I started, but stopped when she glared at me.

The doctors and nurses began coaching her to push and to count to ten, this went on and on. I remained silent, just holding her hand, letting her give me as much pain as she could. I would take it all if I could. I would limit it to only the physical pain labor was creating, not the mental anguish she was suffering.

I lost track of how many times we counted as Christi grew red in the face, while she struggled to push. I did the only thing she would let me, hold her hand and keep quiet. At three seventeen, Christi pushed for the final time and my son entered the world. His skin was coated in a cheese like material the doctor wiped off in a fast motion. She handed me a pair of scissors to cut the umbilical cord, releasing him from his last attachment to his mother. Another nurse whisked him away to the plastic crib with the lights. I leaned down to give my wife a kiss, tell her that I loved her, and thank her for sharing this moment with me. But her eyes were fixed on our son and as soon as she realized what I was doing, she pulled her hand away from me, shooting me death glares once again.

I didn't have any of the evidence here with me, nothing concrete to show her all of this had been just a twisted nightmare. I moved away from the bed and as close as possible to my son. I watched with a protective eye as he was bathed and examined, his cries a sure sign he wasn't happy with the attention he was currently receiving. I wanted to pick him up and take him solidly in my arms. I wanted to give him to his mother for her to give him the type of affection only a mother could bring. But I knew this was all for his own good, just like the medication the nurse was placing in his tiny eyes and the injection she asked Christi about earlier. It was to protect him from outside dangers. I was reminded that it was my job to protect his mother and I'd failed her, twice now. I spun my Claddagh ring and vowed to myself there wouldn't be a third.

"Mr. Malloy, would you like to hold your son?"

The nurse who handed Declan to me was faceless. I didn't know if they were male or female, what kind of car they drove or if they had a family of their own. But in this instant, they were holding a living breathing example of the love his mother and I shared—my son, my first born heir.

With shaking hands and enough adrenaline to kill a horse, I took him from them, being extra careful that his head was guarded and straight. His dark brown hair and tiny nose were like his mother's, but his lips and the shape of his eyes were all me. I tucked him securely into my arms, ready to promise him the world, give him every luxury I could beg, borrow or steal. I was completely in love with this tiny creature and I would kill anyone who tried to hurt him.

Time was an enemy, a thief that would steal how long I got to keep him with me. His mother would demand him soon, how could she not? I knew when she, the gift she had allotted me would be gone and she'd ask me to leave. It was our son who decided when that time was near, he began to fuss and I knew he needed to be with Christi. It didn't help to squelch the yearning I had to crawl into that bed behind her and wrap them both in my arms, daring any motherfucker to take them from me. But his crying increased and I knew my time had expired. Giving him to his mother was easy, natural; it was the letting go of him that about killed me.

"I love you, Declan." I kissed his forehead, then backed away slowly. "Be good for your ma."

I couldn't look at Christi; I knew she would have the same disgusted look on her face that she had the last time I made eye contact with her. My heart just couldn't take it right now. So I left, without a word. I stood with my back to the wall just outside of her room. I could hear her settling the baby and I imagined for just a moment that I was lying there beside her, kissing her cheek, as she touched his face. I pretended that we were happy and she was excited to be my wife.

I failed to notice that Ma was standing beside me. As I opened my eyes, she opened her arms and I fell into her embrace. No words were exchanged, but just like Declan, I needed my ma.

"They're going to move her shortly," Ma whispered in my ear. "Let me get the family here and we'll talk to her as a whole."

I couldn't argue with her; I didn't have much choice left. I nodded my head in silent agreement.

"Call the florist and have him decorate the room. I will phone your da and have him bring what we know."

She kissed my cheek and assured me everything would be all right. I believed her, she was wise and strong and she always kept me doing what I was supposed to do. With her assurance, I almost felt like the clouds were clearing and the sun was about to shine. However, it was the words I heard my wife speak that caused the heavens to open up and pour.

"Gretchen, Declan was born about an hour ago. How fast can we have him served with divorce papers?"

CHAPTER TEN

1 FELT THE ANGER BOILING inside of my chest. She was ready to just toss everything away after hearing only one side of the story. Christi was a member of this family and more importantly, the mother of my new son. She was out of her goddamn mind if she thought for one fucking second that I was going to let her walk away without a fight.

I looked around the hall; I needed reinforcements for what needed to happen. Christi might not want to listen to me, but I had a few people in mind that would make her listen. With no real plan on how to make that happen without the use of violence was foreign territory for me. Give me a gun and I could make any man tell me what I wanted to know, but that beautiful woman, who kept my balls in her purse, wouldn't even look me in the eye, much less spill her guts. I needed to get my shit together before I made her listen.

I removed my phone and sent a text to my men to meet me with the evidence we had, and another to the people I knew she couldn't ignore. Da returned my text that they were on their way and would meet me in the parking lot as they had new information. I didn't like the idea of leaving the floor; I wasn't convinced Christi wouldn't bolt with Declan the first chance she got. However, after the long night I had and the events of the day, I knew I needed sleep. I wasn't about to go home to a house without Christi. A house with no life or laughter, there was only one real choice left.

Not much had changed since I left my parents' house earlier today. The entryway still smelled of the floor cleaner the cleaning service used. The television in my father's study could still be heard, the evening news anchor telling the events of the day, a smile on her face as she shared the doom and gloom of the world around us.

If I could just get a few hours of sleep and a hot shower, I knew I could think of a way to get through to Christi. Ma designed the shower in the guest room with these amazing jets that aligned with your body. I stood with the hot water pulsing at me from three directions, closed my eyes, and let the action calm me. As I ran my towel through my hair, the rumbling of my stomach reminded me I had neglected it for far too long. I wasn't entirely certain when was the last time I ate. There was never a question if there was food prepared in this house. Ma lived to stuff the faces that graced the open doors. I didn't really want to talk with anyone, not until I had a firm idea of what to do about this situation—how to get everyone back under one roof. This time, as I passed my da's study, the door was closed and I assumed my parents had gone up to bed. Sitting in the center of my ma's kitchen island was a plate of meatloaf, steaming hot with a tall frosty glass beside it. I barely even tasted the food as I shoveled it hastily into my mouth, my body acting on its own violation in its need for replenishment.

When I returned, the door to my da's study was open and I could hear the sounds of my da and Sherman talking. I was about to enter the room, when I clearly heard my da talking about a call from McIntyre, our family attorney. I didn't like the tone of his voice, the urgency and, sadly, the fatigue.

"Da, tell me what's going on," I demanded, storming into the room. "What does McIntyre want?" Getting a call from the family attorney was never a good thing, especially with everything going on with Christi.

"Slow down, Patrick," Da cautioned, his stance guarded. "McIntyre was calling to tell me he had an interesting call from an Inspector Beliogini."

I gave him a questioning look as he took a seat and encouraged me to mimic him. "It would appear that Mia Montgomery is singing like a canary in her Italian jail cell." I closed my eyes and settled into the leather chair. Would that nightmare ever die? "She had a lot to say about a certain 'friend' of hers that she recently ended a relationship with." This was the first time I had ever seen Da using air quotes as he spoke. "According to Mia, Theresa Johnson was once her girlfriend."

I looked to Da; his face had the beginnings of a smirk.

"Are you saying . . . ?" The grin formed, no matter how much I tried to fight it.

"Yes, Son, Mia says she's a lesbian."

The urge became too great and the laughter came with an audience as everyone joined me. I could remember Eileen trying to set the two of us up several times over the years. How hard she had worked to place us together. Had I spent any real time with her, I may have been able to hone in on this new detail, save a lot of people a lifetime of heartache.

"She told Beliogini they met a few years ago. Eileen found out and told Mia that Theresa would be the perfect accomplice to their plan to take over."

I was completely awake now. The desire for more clarity raged inside of me, bringing me more strongly into focus.

"How? I mean we never saw her before the open house," I stated, racking my brain, trying to figure out where I had met her prior.

"Oh, but we *did,*" he retorted. His words took on a character full of amusement and fun.

"When, Da? When did I see her?" My tone disbelieving, because frankly I couldn't remember ever noticing her.

Da relaxed into his chair as he took a sip of his drink. "Remember the car that brought Morgan to the wedding?"

My eyes went wide. I had forgotten all about the mystery driver that day. I was so turned on by the way Christi took charge, showing everyone around her that she was secure within herself. She had been more than ready to enter this family and she showed the world just the kind of contender she was inside.

"That was Theresa Johnson?" I verified.

"Mia said she drove the car from the airport to the church and then to an old warehouse where Morgan was killed."

Da and I looked at each other for a few minutes. The pieces of the puzzle started coming together. Each detail brought the big picture more into focus.

"But why did she continue? I mean Eileen is dead and Mia soon will be. There'd be no money coming to her."

"That's where the story takes a little twist," Da said, as he stood and crossed the room. He grabbed a cup from the side board filled with cups and pastries. "It seems that McIntyre also received a call from the Feds."

I knew from earlier that Sherman had some information he hadn't been able to give to me.

"They arrested an Alex Houston. He's a rookie who started with the department about a year ago. He was sitting outside of the church during Books's wedding and decided to follow the car Theresa was driving. He discovered what she was in the process of doing, but she was able to con him into believing she was being forced to do it.

"He took her to his home and she slowly convinced him she had fallen in love with him. He thought he was building a future with her, but she was only using him to get the information she needed on us. She told him she was pregnant with his baby and they needed money to buy a home to raise their family in. He decided if he made a big break in a case against this family that he'd get a promotion and then he could buy them a house.

"So he began to do things on his own time, with no regard for the rules of the department. He made too many mistakes and his department figured out what he was doing. When they arrested him, Theresa laughed in his face and told him she lied about everything, including being pregnant. Apparently, during their pillow talk, Alex spilled a few too many of the Feds' secrets and now she's considered a huge liability. They're asking for our help in putting her away for a long time. They want the video tapes we have."

Sherman and Caleb sat in the corner, silent until this point. Sherman took one look at me and made his way over.

"Patrick, I know who's behind this. I swear we're going to get the truth to Christi. You just need to be ready to take your wife and baby home."

I continued looking at Da's face.

"The condom belonged to an Alex Houston, didn't it . . . ?" Everyone knew it was more of a statement than a question. "I still don't understand why Theresa stayed in the game."

"I think I can help with that one," Caleb announced. "Once Theresa found out Eileen was dead and Mia was in prison, she decided she could still cash in. She used the computer that Alex was issued to hack into our system and steal the video tape she used to trick the monitors. She'd planned to blackmail Patrick with pictures of the hidden panties. Christi just, unfortunately, chose the wrong day to clean the closet."

I turned my attention to Caleb. "How do we know this was her plan?"

Caleb chuckled as he looked me directly in the eye. "Because, Tonto went back to her apartment with Angus and gave her some medication that caused little Theresa to be very truthful."

"Where's the bitch now?" I demanded.

"Right here, Boss," Angus announced, as he shoved a bound and gagged Theresa through the den door.

Her hair was a matted mess and her eyes were black from her running makeup, but she was otherwise unharmed. My guys would never hurt a woman if they didn't have to.

Theresa stumbled and then tripped on the rug. She landed on her side next to the coffee table.

"Sit her up and remove the gag," I ordered. "I want to talk to her."

Tonto put her in the chair and ripped the duct tape off her mouth. I took the chair from the desk and placed it directly in front of her. I said nothing to her as I locked eyes with her. I watched her as she sobbed and squirmed. She never said a word. No one said a word. The only noise in the room was the clicking of the grandfather clock in the hallway. The silence was interrupted by the dinging of all cell phones in the room. I ignored it and continued to stare at her.

She was the reason my life had been upended. She was the reason my wife was thinking I no longer wanted her. I twisted my wedding band as I continued to shoot daggers at her.

I continued to watch Theresa fall apart in the chair. She knew she was caught and she knew she would die soon, yet she said nothing. It only pissed me off further.

"My son was born today." I chose my words carefully. "He's the most beautiful baby I've ever seen."

The tears increased and her entire body trembled. I so wished Christi could see this; could give her everything she deserved for the wrong she had done to this family.

"You took something from me that I'll never get back." Theresa began to shake her head back and forth. "My son was born early and my beautiful wife thinks I was unfaithful because of your lies."

"I-I . . ."

"Did I give you fucking permission to speak to me? You've opened your goddamn mouth too many times when it comes to me!" I shouted at her. Her body began to shake with fear as her sobs increased. "Get this piece of shit out of my sight!" I threw my phone at her.

"Patrick," Ma's soft voice spoke.

I turned and came face to face with nearly the entire family. Ammo stood in front of Muscles and a very pregnant Amex stood holding Sherman and Caleb's hands. However, Smiles's face was the one that caught my attention. "She never left my side when Abby was born." I crossed the room and took Smiles into a tight hug. "It's supposed to be a magical time, having your first baby."

"Theresa took that from her," I spoke into her ear.

"She took it from you as well," Smiles responded.

"I know . . . I know."

"We're going to get her back, get her to listen to reason," Smiles assured me, stroking my face. "She may not listen to you, but she will listen to me."

It was a little later when everyone left. I had found a chair on the patio that was quiet and alone. I sat out there for hours and thought about everything that had happened. I replayed the memories of meeting my Christi, falling madly in love with her, taking her to my bed for the first time, dancing with her, waking up with her, begging for her forgiveness . . . watching my son being born.

I heard the patio door open and got a whiff of Ma's perfume. I felt her warm hand on my shoulder as she walked around the chair.

"She believed a lie, Ma."

"I know, sweetheart."

"After all the times I've told her how much I love her, that I'd never be unfaithful, she still believed a fucking lie."

Ma placed her warm hand on my knee. I knew her words of wisdom were about to make the hurt go away, just like she did when I was a little boy and fell and scraped my knees—if only it was that easy.

"You have a big choice to make. You can either dwell on the negative of this or you can rejoice in knowing she's safe and he's healthy."

I knew she was right. Once Christi heard the truth, she would apologize and promise to make it up to me. I knew that wasn't what I wanted.

"I need to see my son," I spoke, as I rose from the chair and headed upstairs to shower.

Last night when Smiles had shared her plan, I could have kissed her. Actually, that was exactly what I did—it was her cheek—but I still kissed her in appreciation. The plan was simple. Christi wanted nothing to do with me or any male member of the family, but she could never refuse her sister, or mine, for that matter. Ammo would go along as the muscle in the situation. The ladies would enter her room, while I waited—not so patiently outside the door—listening for my cue to come in. With my back pressed to the same spot I found last night, I closed my eyes and prayed this plan would work.

"You know when you look into the store window of a pet shop and you see all of the cute and cuddly puppies playing with one another, then you take one home just to find out he pisses on the floor and chews up your best pair of heels?"

The girls entered the room a united front. I listened carefully as Ma stood beside me. I could just picture them standing with arms cross and glaring at Christi; somehow I knew she would be glowing sitting in that hospital room.

"I say we take the baby and leave his mom to wallow in the hole she's dug for herself," Amex suggested.

"No, Patrick would kill us for that. However, she's going to owe us big after this." Smiles said; her voice laden with attitude that only a sister, who was about to hand you your ass, could carry.

"Don't you roll your eyes at me, Christi!" Smiles suddenly barked. I adjusted my position, struggling not to laugh.

I could hear their clicking of heels as they moved around the room, surely getting closer to Christi's bed.

"Give my nephew to me," Amex demanded.

"Oh, Sissy, what am I going to do with you?"

The sounds of sobs followed and I knew they were from my wife. I had to physically hold on to the wall to keep from dashing in there and holding her.

"Don't worry; you've got us and we'll help you fix this," Ammo instructed. Her voice was muffled; she must have been hugging a crying Christi. I could hear Declan begin to fuss and I yearned to soothe him.

"Christi, I swear to God, I love you like no other, but this is beyond belief. If you hadn't just given birth to the most beautiful baby, I'd totally kick your skinny ass." Ammo spoke loud and clear. I made out the sounds of sniffles that I couldn't assign, but assumed whom they belonged to.

"I knew the two of you would make beautiful babies, but he's more perfect than I imagined. He looks exactly like Patrick," Amex said, admiration in her voice.

The sounds of crying began again.

"Well, I'm certain he and Theresa will have plenty of beautiful . . ."

Christi's voice cut off, she was crying I was more than certain. It was killing me to stand here against this wall and do nothing.

"Oh, my fucking, God!" Ammo exclaimed.

"Allyson, watch your language," Smiles corrected.

"Sorry, Declan, but get used to that word, your daddy invented it," Ammo tossed.

"I cannot believe you just walked away from him like that." Ammo was pissed. I'd seen her take on women who eyed up Muscles a time or two, broke a few noses in her early days.

"Oh, no you don't! He left me. He chose that fucking bitch over his wife and baby!" Christi shot back.

"Are you serious? You honestly believe the word of that whore over your own husband's?" It was my sister this time, asking the same question I had asked myself repeatedly the past two days.

"Ugh,"Christi moaned.

"Christi?" Smiles's voice was full of concern.

"I'm all right," Christi assured, her voice frail and weak.

"No, you're not all right, Christi. You've lost your fucking mind if you think for one second he fucked Theresa." Smiles was locked and loaded; Christi would have no choice but to listen. This was the plan we had discussed. I leaned back again, listening. I knew Smiles would use the sister card, Christi would have no defense against it.

"No, you sit and listen to me!" Smiles shouted. "I know you. You've always been the stronger one of the two of us. You've always told me not to put up with shit from anyone. But what you've done to that man, and that little boy, is beyond standing up for yourself."

"Get out," Christi spoke with vehemence. "Get your shit and get the fuck out!"

"Shut the fuck up, Christi! I'll leave after you've listened to everything I have to say."

"Patrick has done nothing but worship the motherfucking ground you walk on since the day he married you. How the fuck you can just toss him away on the word of a lying, backstabbing bitch, is beyond me?"

I could hear movement again. Smiles had taken a black bag into the room with her; it contained copies of everything we had against Theresa. The loud slamming of a hand against a table was followed by the rustling of papers . . . then complete and tortuous silence.

I waited, breath held and a few Hail Marys silently recited in my head. This was it, either she looked at the evidence and tossed it out or she pulled her head out of her ass and believed us . . . in us.

"Oh, my God! I divorced him over a lie."

The room filled with laughter, my face contorted in confusion as to why they felt any of this was funny.

"Well, you nearly divorced him. Lucky for you, I've known McIntyre's daughter for several years. She called me the second you called about filing the papers."

"She never even filed the papers. But that's the least of your worries," Amex spoke.

"I need to call my da." I was about to go into the room and put an end to all of this nonsense.

The slapping of skin halted me in my tracks. I didn't know if they hit her or not, I just knew I needed to get in there and fast.

"No, you need to call your husband!" Smiles spoke, her voice angry again.

"Really, Shannon? Call the man who, as you three just reminded me, I've thrown away? Do you think he's just going to waltz into this room and throw his arms around me and life will be the way it was before I confronted him?"

I could hear Declan beginning to fuss again, the rustle of blankets and then, "How do you know, Christi?" Ammo questioned.

"We all know what he'll do, Allyson."

"Listen, the last time I saw Patrick, he was pulling at his hair and trying to figure out how to get you to listen to him."

It was time for ma to join them. With a kiss to my cheek, she entered the room. She would take in Christi's condition and then give me the cue to enter.

"Good morning, my sweethearts. Oh, goodness, what is this?" she questioned.

"Hey, Ma," Ammo spoke as she kissed her cheek.

"Not much, just opening my sister's eyes," Smiles said, *her* voice at least sounded happy.

"Ah, and did we like what we saw, Christi?"

I couldn't speak. I could only hold my breath as I waited for Ma to say the magic word. To let me know that she felt everything was all right enough for me to come in and fix this; to claim my family again.

"Christi, let me have Declan before you hurt him." Regardless of what Ma said, Christi would never hurt our son.

"Good morning, my sweet baby," she cooed. "Christi, you didn't answer my question," Ma spoke, as the sound of the tape that held his diaper on being pulled away. She must be changing him, something I was longing to do.

"No, Nora . . . I didn't like what I saw." Christi's voice was drained, she was tired and hurt. Something I could fix in an instant.

"Neither did Patrick when he saw her in that picture." I closed my eyes as I imagined Christi looking at the picture of Theresa in the nursery.

"What did he say?" Her voice sounded muffled as if she had something like a pillow over it.

"Well, why don't you ask him yourself? He's waiting in the hall-way."

CHAPTER ELEVEN

THE SIGHT BEFORE ME WOULD forever be etched into my memory. Ma stood holding my son, lovingly cooing to him. Smiles stood in the corner of the room, anger written across her face, a lone tear cascading down her cheek. Amex and Ammo were examining the gifts that littered the corner of the room. Finally, there was my Christi, sitting in the middle of the hospital bed, her hair a disheveled mess, her eyes ringed in soft purple and swollen, with red-tinged rims. It was clear she had been crying; her eyes immediately cast down when she saw me, as if she was ashamed.

"Well, hello, Daddy."

Ma continued to rock my son as she made her way over to me. I held out my arms as she placed his warm bundle into my hands. In the instant I drew him to my chest, my purpose in life changed. I could feel the energy that resonated from him. He was a product of the undying love Christi and I shared. He was a miracle and I would protect him until my last breath. I would give him the world. I would be the example of the man he needed to grow up to be.

"I'll just leave the two of you alone," Ma whispered into my ear as she gently kissed my cheek.

It was as if no one else mattered to me in the world. I ran my eyes up and down his perfect face. I would never tire of looking at him. The absolute infinite amount of love I had for him consumed me, threatening to take over my very soul.

"Hello, little man," I whispered as he began to wiggle and stretch. I had to laugh at the expressions he had as he raised his tiny arms beside his head. "It's your daddy again." I placed gentle kisses on his forehead and cheeks. "You have no idea much I've missed you."

I closed my eyes and brought his head to my chin. I inhaled his intoxicating baby scent and suddenly everything was right with the world. I softly told him that I would teach him how to play football and how to use his Malloy charm to win over all the girls. How his grandparents were waiting to spoil him rotten. How I would always be there for him as my father had been for me. I told him so many things. And I swore I would do everything in my power to give him all he needed, starting with a happy mommy.

I would teach him by example. Yes, I was a mob boss, but that didn't mean I couldn't teach him the core values of being a good man, a good husband, and father. That was my job and it would start today.

Declan began to fuss, while sucking his fist, and I suspected he might be hungry. It was confirmed when I looked up and watched as Christi unsnapped her hospital gown and bra. The sight of her took my breath away. She had always been beautiful, but today, even though she was sad and clearly tired, she was still the most beautiful girl in my world.

I kissed little Declan's head as I carefully handed him to his mother. You would have thought Christi had been nursing all her life and not a mere day.

I sat beside her and gently ran my finger along his brown hair.

"I want to tell you I'm sorry, but I know you're tired of hearing that from me." Her voice was so small and whisper soft.

"You're right, Christi. I don't want to hear I'm sorry from you."

I tried to keep my emotions in check; she didn't need to be upset by harsh words while she was feeding the baby. I continued to watch as she fed Declan, and she would whisper kind words to him as she rubbed his tiny cheek. When she switched from one breast to the other, she did so with the ease of someone who had done this for years. Declan took her nipple into his mouth as if it were a lifeline. I stroked his pink cheek gently and chuckled as I told him, "Just remember, Son, those were mine first and they're only on loan. I want them back when you're finished."

I watched as he continued to nurse. Christi's eyes never left Declan's face. This was my family, my responsibility.

"I was about to call my dad when you came in," Christi explained as she removed a sleeping Declan from her chest.

I took him from her, crossed the room, and placed him back in his crib. I stood over him, watching him sleep. I wanted to be like him, a full belly and not a care in the world; completely loved and protected.

"Has Matthew seen him yet?"

"No." Her voice was so soft, so frail.

I turned my eyes to her. "Why not?" I asked, my brow wrinkling in confusion.

I watched as her shoulders sank, her head once again lowering, a lone tear falling down her face. I held my place, giving her space to get her thoughts together. If I had learned anything about my wife, it was that sometimes it was best to let her have her say.

"I realize that with everything that's happened in the past couple of days, it's probably best I take Declan to my dad's house. Until I can get on my feet, that is."

With a quick glance at my sleeping son, I made my way back toward Christi.

"Well, if you think we'll need extra hands, I'm certain Ma and Charlotte would be happy to alternate staying with us."

Christi's head snapped up and her eyes locked with mine. "Y-you s-said . . . us," Christi mumbled.

"I did, as in you and me. Declan has two parents, last time I checked." I couldn't help but give her a half-grin.

"But . . . I . . . how . . . ?"

I had never seen Christi as confused as she currently was. A small part of me was enjoying having the upper hand; okay, a large part of me, but only because it didn't happen very often.

"Christi, I think it's time you heard the entire story about Theresa."

I crossed the remaining three feet and settled on the bed beside her. I took her hand in mine and began to tell her the events that had been told to me. Christi never moved or said a single word as I explained everything.

I kissed her temple and rubbed the back of her hand as she took it all in. Her bewildered look rapidly changed to one of anger. She began to shake her head.

"I feel so stupid." She tilted her head back and let out a deep sigh. "She would constantly throw out little quips . . . but . . ." She waved her hands around, trying to find her words. "I always just shrugged it off as her venting because of her husband, Alex."

"What kinds of things?" I would kill Theresa myself if she had upset my wife.

"Just stuff like how handsome you are and how if you were her husband, she wouldn't let you get dressed. Crazy things like that." She looked into my eyes then steadied herself. "I know you don't want excuses for my very poor behavior, but honestly, I'm at a loss here. I don't know how to fix it or that you even want to fix it."

I smiled as I took her face in my hands. I softly kissed her nose and touched my forehead to hers. I took a deep breath and relished in her warm scent, it grounded me, prepared me for what I needed to say.

"Last night, when I found out the truth, I went through so many emotions. Ma reminded me that I could take this as a bump in the road of our marriage or I could choose to make it a wall and end it. I sat outside last night and thought over everything we've been through. I remembered how hard I worked to earn your heart. How I swore to God that if he brought you back to me after you were kidnapped, I would let you see how much I really loved you. I'd do everything in my power to keep you."

I closed my eyes and kissed her pink lips. Oh, how I had missed kissing her.

"Honestly, Christi, at one point last night, I thought about letting you suffer with your actions, but then I realized by doing that, I'm punished as well. The way I see it, I have to take the good and the bad of the hormones you have running around in your body. The good was when you couldn't get enough of me, and as much as I truly enjoyed it, it's time to pay the price."

I looked into her eyes; I could still see the doubt weighing heavily on her mind.

"Christi, I know you have so many emotions running through you right now. I wish you could crawl into my head, my heart, and see how deeply I feel for you. Babe, I have everything I want in this room. I have no desire to ever be away from either of you."

I kissed her again and tried to show her all the love I still had for her.

"Patrick, I know that you're telling me the truth . . . I-I just . . ." She lowered her eyes and shook her head back and forth.

I had to make her see this was real. That my devotion to her and our son was real and she didn't have to question me or my feelings for her.

I looked down at my hands that were holding her delicate ones. I watched as her engagement ring sparkled from the overhead lights, how it cast various rainbows as she moved her tiny finger. I wondered briefly when she had put it back on. I watched as the glint from my own ring cast its own rays. Then it hit me, the Claddagh.

"Christi, do you remember when I gave you the shamrock necklace?"

She moved her eyes to mine and nodded her head.

"Do you remember what I told you about it?"

I watched as her left hand reached up and she placed the tips of her fingers over where it used to rest, as if to pull the memory to the front of her mind.

"You said it was to let people know that we were together, so no other man would come on to me."

I smiled at her response. She was right; I had been pretty caveman about the explanation I gave her.

"Yes, I do remember telling you that." I chuckled mostly to myself as I continued. "Do you remember the first morning we woke up after the wedding and you noticed the Claddagh I wear on my pinky?"

Her face looked puzzled as she again nodded her head.

"Christi, what I'm about to tell you is something that you must swear to keep to yourself. No one can ever know that you know this."

I watched as her eyes darted frantically back and forth between mine.

"The shamrock was a promise, but the Claddagh holds so much more."

I looked down at my ring and twisted it around my finger, remembering the moment my father placed it on my finger, binding the vow I took.

"When I gave you the shamrock, I gave you my word that I was devoted to you and only you. With that shamrock, you carried my vow of being true to you. The Claddagh represents the vow I took with my father and the married men of my family. A vow that I would never dishonor you in any way."

The room was silent as I continued to look at my ring. The tradition dated back further than anyone knew.

"This vow that you took . . ." Her voice was riddled with emotion, cracking at the end. "If . . . if you were to break it, what would happen?"

I looked her straight in the eye as I responded. "My father would have to kill me."

I watched her as her eyes went wide and her loud gasp echoed in the quiet room.

"Thomas wouldn't really . . ."

I sat up straighter and took her whole body in my arms.

"He would have, Christi. He asked me if I had done anything. When I told him no, he worked very hard to help me prove it."

I released her as she pushed at my chest.

"Will our son make that same vow?" Her eyes were pleading with mine.

"Yes, Christi. Every Malloy man makes that vow."

Christi rose from the bed, crossing the room to Declan's cradle. "I can't imagine him all grown up and getting married."

I stood and moved in behind her, wrapping my arms around her middle.

"One day, he'll find a young woman who completes him as you complete me. He'll give her the shamrock and, on his wedding day, I'll pass the Claddagh to him."

Christi turned in my arms, wrapped her arms around my middle, and snuggled her face into my chest.

"I wish you hadn't told me that. I know why you did, but I wish it didn't come to this." I turned my face into her hair, kissing the top of her head. "Tell me how to make this better, Patrick."

I stood and held her for the longest time, swaying back and forth. This idea actually came to me last night.

"I only want one thing from you to call us even."

Her head snapped up, her eyes once again locked with mine.

"I'll do just about anything. Please, tell me." Her eyes pleading, her lower lip quivering

"When you have your final checkup with your doctor, I want to get pregnant again as fast as possible. I want another baby as soon as we can."

She didn't blink an eye as she responded. "You actually read my mind. I was just thinking that very same thing."

I smiled as I kissed her with all the passion I felt for her.

Six weeks. The countdown had begun . . .

Chapter Twelve

HE MONTH FOLLOWING DECLAN'S BIRTH was filled with event after event. I refused to allow Christi to do anything except nurse him and rest. Smiles had asked us to be little Michael's godparents and the christening was upon us. Father Murphy was gracious enough to do Declan's blessing before we left the hospital.

Ma pulled me aside and questioned whether I'd thought about selling the house and buying a new one. She was concerned that Christi would have too many bad memories. Christi, however, dismissed the idea and refused to let Theresa win. She had never backed down from a fight and refused to let this one be the first.

Christi was going with Ma today to get little Michael his first crucifix. I had informed the jeweler to give Christi anything she wanted. I had also given him strict instructions to start Christi a special bracelet that contained Declan's birthstone. I would give it to her after Declan's christening.

The idea of having a double christening was put on the table, and just as quickly, squashed. Ma felt it was important to celebrate each birth independently. No one dared argue, so the plan was to have them a week apart.

We were still having trouble with that group of punks who had continued to terrorize the neighborhood. One of the ladies from the bakery not far from Christi's old office called Da and asked for help.

Mrs. O'Leary was the sweetest, little old lady I had ever met. She was also not one to let young kids get away with anything. I remembered her yanking on my ear quite a few times while I was growing up. She also made the most amazing chocolate chip cookies. Those cookies had kids fighting over who would sweep her front steps on a daily basis.

I'd sent Tonto and Shamus over there, but the only thing they had managed to do was come home with bellies full of said cookies. Da called me last night and told me we would be making a special visit to her shop today.

Christi opened the door and greeted Da with a warm hug. He immediately pulled Declan from her arms and tossed him into the air. Declan squealed with glee, while Christi gasped in horror.

"Oh, now don't fret, little Christi. I did this to all my kids and they're perfectly fine."

My wife, however, was never one not to have a word to add, responded, "Well, that definitely explains several things that are odd about your son."

Declan was still laughing as Da looked oddly at her, taking in her comment and trying not to laugh, I could safely assume. Christi never missed a beat, asking if he would like something to drink, while taking Declan back into her arms. He declined, of course. Declan fussed for a minute until Christi excused herself to go and nurse him.

I told Da I would meet him in his car and made my way to the nursery to say goodbye to my family. Watching Christi rock and nurse

Declan was a sight I wanted to forever hold in my mind. I smiled at the sight of them together, the rocking chair gently swaying as she sat confidently and hummed to him. Over the past six weeks, Christi had slowly returned to the Christi I'd fallen in love with. Her confidence level had returned and she was once again even-tempered. She had also been driving me crazy with need every time she paraded around our bedroom naked, her gloriously full nursing breasts on display. Sometimes, I would swear she did it on purpose, forbidden fruit as the big exam had not happened, yet.

Her eyes left our son's face and locked with mine. Her smile was huge and genuine.

"You do remember that I have my check up today, right?" she questioned, her eyes turning dark with lust.

I could only smile at her. She had definitely been doing the naked parade on purpose.

"Why, Mrs. Malloy, are you suggesting something?"

Her coyness was refreshing as she switched breasts. Her bottom lip became a prisoner of her teeth as her eyes again met mine beneath her thick lashes.

"I'm suggesting that you should make certain you're home before I fall asleep this evening."

I chuckled as I took in her Cheshire grin.

"It's a date, Mrs. Malloy."

Growing up, I learned that you could tell what kind of mood my father was in by what car he chose to drive. As I exited the house, I instantly knew this would be an interesting day as he sat behind the wheel of his brand new Chevy Camaro. Ma had mumbled something in Gaelic that I didn't quite catch and knew I didn't want to. When he had brought this car, he was in the mood to fight.

He didn't even give me time to fasten my seat belt, before he peeled out of my driveway. I buckled up and then threw on my shades, placing a new attitude behind the lenses.

"Damn it, old man! If you get me killed, Christi is gonna kick your ass."

He only huffed as he pressed the gas pedal harder.

"Six weeks are just about up, aren't they?" he asked, as he plugged in his iPod.

"As a matter of fact, Christi goes to the doctor today."

"That's what your ma said. She didn't sleep last night and was up all night getting the house ready for Declan."

I smiled as I looked out the side window. Ma had volunteered to keep Declan for us any time we wanted her to. Christi had suggested that she keep him while she went to the doctor's office and maybe did a little shopping. Ma had cleared her schedule and had been working hard to convert one of the bedrooms into a nursery and playroom. Judging by my father's admission, she had put things into high gear.

It wasn't long before my father pulled along the curb in front of Mrs. O'Leary's shop. Not much had changed since the last time I'd visited. Mr. O'Leary had passed away several years prior. Their son, Sean, had come home and painted the outside of the building, but he had no desire to work in the bakery and his wife refused to move to the big city. Mrs. O'Leary never batted an eye as she continued to run the bakery by herself.

I could remember my mother ordering all of our birthday cakes from here and I knew she'd already ordered the cakes for the up-coming christenings last week. I paused as I reached for the door of the bakery. I noticed a car slowly coming down the street, its stereo thumping. My grandfather used to say that the speakers in these people's cars were worth more than the whole car. I chuckled as I removed my shades and stepped into the shop.

Once inside, I felt like a ten-year-old boy again. The smell of fresh bread, sugar, and spices engulfed me. Once Declan was older, I would bring him here. I wanted him to have great memories to pass along to his own son.

"Well, would ya look at what the wind blew in."

I smiled as Mrs. O'Leary stood behind the counter, her hair still bright red and her lipstick matched. Her white frilly apron wrapped around her neck without a spot of dirt on it. Her eyes were bright as she made her way around the counter, headed for Da.

Da was a good two feet taller than her, but she still managed to bring his face down to her level and kissed each of his cheeks.

"Mr. Malloy, how are ya this fine mornin'?" She said in her thick Irish accent.

"I'd be perfect if you'd call me Thomas," he corrected, then kissed her cheeks in return.

"Oh, now, and are me old eyes deceiving me?" She turned to my direction.

"No, Mrs. O'Leary." I smiled as I made my way over to her. She might have been a small woman, but she could hug like a grizzly bear.

"Where's that new baby of yours? Home with his ma as he should be, I'd imagine."

I smiled and nodded as she took my face in her hands, kissing both my cheeks as well.

"I want to see that new baby, ya hear me?"

"Yes, Ma'am. I'll tell Christi we need to come visit."

"Not too soon, mind ya. Ya keep that baby wrapped up tight.

Keep the evil spirits away until he's blessed, good and proper, in the church."

Mrs. O'Leary was a good woman, but she believed in the old ways. In her time, things were done differently. I would have to be careful what I did or said around her today.

"Now, let me get ye gentlemen something good and nourishing into ya."

She moved behind the counter and began making a pot of tea and arranging different pastries on a platter.

It wasn't until she moved behind the counter that I noticed a pretty blonde-haired girl arranging bread in the display. Her blonde hair was pulled tight into a ponytail, her skin very fair and her clothes quite minimal. She reminded me of Christi at an early age, minus the dark hair of course. She was clearly shy since she refused to make eye contact with me.

I joined my father at one of the little café tables that sat in the shop.

"Megan, be a dear and take this to the Malloy men."

The shy girl complied, but she kept her head down as she placed the tray on our table.

"Thank you, Megan," Da told her.

She only smiled and abruptly left to return to her work. Once she was behind the counter, Mrs. O'Leary, with a cup of tea in her hand, joined us at the table.

"Thomas, I cannot tell ya how good it does me poor old soul to see ya here today."

"It's my honor."

"Poor Megan, just hasn't been the same since the last time those hooligans came into me shop. Had to pull out me shotgun, I did."

I could just picture her with a big old, rusty gun that she more than likely brought over from Ireland with her. I, for one, wouldn't want to be on the receiving end of that gun.

"Can you tell us what happened?"

She took a sip of her tea as she began her story.

"Megan came to me nearly eight months ago. She didn't have two nickels to rub together and had a new wee one to feed. She came into me shop to get out of the rain and I offered her a cup of tea. She told me she didn't have any money, so I told her it was an old pot and I would have to be rid of it, anyway."

I looked at the shy girl again. She looked like she hadn't had a good night's sleep in weeks, months maybe.

"I offered her a job here and a place to stay in Sean's old room. I couldn't ask for a better worker and the poor baby, quiet as a church mouse."

"Did she mention where the baby's father was?" my father questioned.

"She told me he'd run off in the night. Left her with not a dime or a care." She shook her head as she took another sip of her tea.

My cell phone vibrated in my pocket. I retrieved it to find a text from Tonto.

My brother, Dustin, is in town. He's looking for work. Can I put him to work at the club?

I typed a reply.

Bring him to the bakery, I want to talk to him myself first.

I placed my phone back in my pocket as I looked around the room. Da continued to talk about the punks who had been harassing the local businesses. She told us of the last time they had been in this shop. Seemed they had scared Megan so bad that Mrs. O'Leary was convinced she would turn and run. She said that the ringleader had taken a fancy to Megan and would touch her in a way that wasn't appropriate. Megan had been so scared she cried for hours after they left.

"Thomas, I don't worry about me self so much, but Megan has been through too much and I fret that this will cause her harm."

Da only shook his head as he continued to drink his tea.

I noticed that my black SUV had pulled up behind my father's car. Tonto exited first, followed by a dark-haired man I remembered from when Christi was kidnapped. They rounded the car, pulled out a cigarette, and began to smoke. He got points from me for doing that outside and away from the store.

The bell over the door chimed, as a group of men entered the shop.

"Sweet Jesus, Mary, and Joseph," Mrs. O'Leary spoke, her tone exasperated.

I looked back at the men who had walked into the shop. The first was wearing his hat backwards, his hair looked to be slicked back with either too much gel or not enough soap. It looked like he was trying to grow some facial hair, but his punk-ass balls hadn't dropped yet, so he wasn't having any luck. His tennis shoes were untied and his jeans were six sizes too big for him. He was trying hard to look like a gangster, but failing miserably. I had seen his type countless times; trying to be a badass, only managing to break a few laws and ending up with a record. The bitches who followed behind him looked exactly the same.

The leader moved calculatedly around the counter and stood there, waiting for poor Megan to look up.

"How can I help you gents today?" Mrs. O'Leary questioned, confidence and strength in her voice.

"I came to talk to my girl today," he replied, his voice full of arrogance, his eyes never leaving Megan. His smile was sinister and

I could almost see, by the way he licked his lips, the plans he had for her.

Da stood and made his way over the group of men, his cup still in his hand.

"Yes, well, the young lady isn't on the menu. Try picking something that is or get the hell out."

The young punk only snickered as he reached for Megan's hand. She stood trembling as her eyes danced from the punk to my father.

"Mind your own business, old man," the punk tossed back at Da.

The bell above the door chimed again as Tonto and Dustin came into the bakery. I made eye contact with Tonto and gave him a warning look. He closed the door and placed his arms across his chest, Dustin followed suit.

Megan had looked to see who had entered and locked eyes with Dustin.

"I told you I'd be back for you," the punk told Megan. "I know you missed me, baby? Why you frontin'?"

Megan's eyes never left Dustin's and, for a second, I wondered if Dustin was her baby's father. The look they had for each other was off. It wasn't with surprise or distaste, it was with wonder and intrigue.

Da stepped closer, once again warning the punk. "I won't tell you again, the lady isn't here for you."

The punk then turned his attention to Da and attempted to grab his shirt. I said attempted because quicker than you could blink, Da had the punk's face slammed into the wooden countertop, blood gushing from his broken nose. Dustin jumped the counter and had Megan wrapped in his arms, kissing the top of her hair.

I pulled my gun and had the remaining punks with their hands held in the air. Tonto had his gun to the back of one of the remaining punk's heads, daring him to move a muscle.

Da jerked the guy's hair back and held his face where he could talk to him.

"I won't tell you this twice, get the hell out of this neighborhood and don't come back! If you do, I'll personally place a fucking bullet in your fucking brain. You got me, motherfucker?"

He didn't give him a chance to answer, as he tossed his body to his gang. Tonto opened the door and began shoving the men out, one by one. Dustin continued to hold tightly to a sobbing Megan.

By the time we left the bakery, I had a new employee, Da had two boxes of cookies, and Dustin had a dinner date with Megan. All in all, it had been a hell of a day.

We headed to the office to tie up a few loose ends. By the time we had everything in order, it was close to eight o'clock in the evening. Da dropped me off at my house and wished me a goodnight. I had no doubt it would be.

I secured the door, set the alarm, and made my way up the stairs and into Declan's room.

He was tucked in his crib, sleeping away. I leaned over and kissed his chubby cheeks. He woke up momentarily and must have mistaken me for Christi, as he tried to suck on my nose. I chuckled at him and placed his pacifier in his mouth. He fell back to sleep instantly. Guess ma wasn't keeping him tonight; maybe the word from the doctor wasn't good. Maybe she wasn't fully healed. I would wait, blue balls and all.

I removed my jacket as I entered our bedroom. I froze in my tracks when I found my beautiful wife sprawled across the bed. She had the sexiest and tightest corset on. It was black with red bows down the front; the matching garter had the same bows and held her black stockings in place. Thank God she had forgotten to put on the matching panties.

"Hello, honey." Her voice was low and sexy. My mouth refused to work as I stood there staring at her bare core. "Hello . . . my eyes are up here." She snapped her fingers, bringing my attention to her eyes.

"Well, this is a surprise." My voice sounded foreign even to me.

"I got the green light from my doctor today."

I crossed the room and placed my body atop hers, my lips claimed hers as my hips ground into her.

"Ugh," she moaned.

"Baby, I have missed this," I spoke into her neck as I nipped and sucked. "It's been too fucking long."

I moved my hands to her satin and lace-covered breasts. I didn't want to get them leaking, but damn it, I missed them.

"Oh, yes," she purred.

I moved my mouth to the top of her breast where I licked, kissed, massaged and worshipped.

"Please tell me you got this fucking thing on sale?" I questioned as I tried to take the thing off of her.

"N-No, I paid far too much for it."

I didn't give a fuck if she'd paid ten thousand dollars for it, it was in my way. I took the cloth in my hands and split it down the middle. Once her breasts were uncovered, I took them into my hands, my lips and teeth teasing her nipples. Needing to feel her skin against me, I ditched my clothes as my cock sprang to life.

I had to slow down, it had been so long and I hoped that she had recovered fully from giving birth to our son. Would she feel the same? Did we have any lube? Maybe I should just get her off a few times and then have her give me a hand job. My eagerness decreased, but I should have known that Christi would notice I was having this internal battle. I had to be gentle, make sure she was loved properly.

"Patrick, I'm not a china doll that will break if you touch me. I need you to let go, feel me for once. I want you to lose control, I need this."

I looked into her hazel eyes;, they told me everything I needed to know. She needed me to show her the side of me that I had hidden from her up until now. Without a second thought, I grabbed her hip, and flipped her over.

"You should be careful what you wish for," I growled as I entered her roughly. "You just might get it."

I watched as my cock slid in and out of her, wet with her arousal. Her pussy was tighter than I remembered.

"Harder, Patrick!" she cried.

I gripped her hip with one hand and wrapped her hair around the other. I began to slam into her with such gusto, that you could hear our bodies slapping against each other. Our breathing was labored and her moans grew bolder.

"Oh yes . . . just like that!" she shouted.

I let go of her hair, reached around, and pinched her swollen clit. I could feel my balls slamming into her lips as I continued to thrust into her, hard and fast.

"Ohhhh!" she chanted as I felt her walls begin to vibrate around me. I was far from done with her, but I let her orgasm finish before I wrapped my arms around her tiny waist and took her across the room, placing her against the wall. I didn't give her a second to recover, before I slid inside her again. Her legs wrapped around my waist as she began to cry out my name over and again over.

She was right, I needed this. I'd always been so careful with her, always making it a point to be a tender lover. But, goddamn, it felt so good to just fuck her.

"Patrick . . . I-I oh, God . . . right oh . . . oh . . . oh . . ." She couldn't even finish her sentence as her second orgasm rocked her body. Her face and neck flushed and her eyes closed as she savored the feelings and the emotions.

Her forehead hit my shoulder and she was panting so heavily. I continued to pound her into the wall.

"You like that, baby? You like me fucking your perfect pussy?"

Her head raised and the look on her face nearly did me in.

"My turn," she spoke as she removed her legs from around me, causing my dick to slip out of her.

Christi shoved me back toward the bed, straddled my hips, and slammed her wet pussy down on my hard cock. I watched in awe as her breasts bounced as she rode me hard. I was losing the battle to hold off my climax. She looked just too good riding me for all she was worth.

I looked down and watched as my cock disappeared into her warm core every time she moved, over me. However, when Christi placed her fingers on her clit, I lost the battle.

The combination of my climax and Christi's fingers brought her to a finish as well.

We lay side by side, sweating and panting, while as we tried to catch our breath.

"Baby, I think there's a good chance you knocked the balls off our next child. It will probably be a girl."

I wanted more children with her;, we had discussed this at great length. Just to be certain we did conceive, I took her three more times that night. After all, she wanted a girl.

Chapter Thirteen

"**1** BAPTIZE YOU IN THE name of the Father, the Son, and the Holy Spirit. Amen."

I stood proudly beside my beautiful wife. Her hair was pulled back into a low ponytail, teasing me with her soft creamy neck. I shouldn't have been having these thoughts here in the middle of church, during my son's baptism, but I wanted her, I always wanted her.

Ever since Christi's checkup, we had been tearing each other's clothes off as often as possible.

Declan's baptism drew in more people than our wedding. Ma had insisted Maggie help plan the event, and looking at the number in attendance, I was glad she had.

Christi decided she wanted to have Angus and Maggie as Declan's godparents. She wanted someone outside of the immediate family so that no feelings were hurt. I knew Angus and Maggie would raise our son in the proper manner, if the need arose.

Declan didn't move a muscle as the priest trickled the holy water over his forehead. Maggie was waiting with a towel and a new diaper once the priest was done.

I could hear the voices of some of Ma's friends talking about how calm the baby was and how that was a sign of a good leader. I silently chuckled. Ma had just told Christi I was so upset during my christening I screamed the whole time and then peed on my god-mother. I guessed I wasn't such a good leader after all.

Once the ceremony was over and the reception had begun, Da pulled me aside and asked if I had shared Theresa's fate with Christi. I smiled and rubbed my thumb along my bottom lip as I recalled the conversation we'd had one night after we'd placed our son in his crib.

"Patrick, I want to ask you a question and I really need to know the truth; even if you don't want to share it with me."

I looked at Christi and then took her by the hand, leading her to the living room. I curled around her and softly traced my fingers alongside of her.

"I wondered when you were going to ask me this."

Christi turned and looked at me with her big, expressive eyes. Her fingers softly caressed my stubble that I had decided against shaving that morning.

"She's dead isn't she?"

Christi's voice was full of emotion, which surprised me. Theresa had caused us so much pain and nearly cost us our marriage. My wife had a pure heart and this was evident in her words.

"No, my love, she isn't dead. Not that I didn't consider it."

Christi's eyes became huge and she turned fully in my lap.

"Then . . . what?"

I eased her back on the couch, kissing her warm, pink lips.

"We decided to cooperate with the Feds on this one."

Christi looked more confused than ever. She opened and closed her mouth several times.

I kissed her forehead and snuggled in beside her. I had my hand in her hair, letting the silky strands fall between my fingers.

"Babe, sometimes doing the right thing in this family doesn't require a bullet." I tilted my head against hers as I closed my eyes and continued. "We decided to cooperate with the Feds and turned her over, along with the tapes from the security footage. In exchange, they managed to get a virus in their evidence files against us."

"So, she's behind bars now?"

"Yes, Christi. She's behind bars for the crimes she committed against the government."

Christi took a deep breath and then let out the cutest hum.

"Someday I'll forgive her, not today, but someday."

I opened my eyes, turned, and kissed her head again.

"I'm glad one of us will."

"I don't even have to ask if she was comfortable with our decision, do I, Son?" Da chuckled as he took a drink of his scotch.

"You'd be wasting your breath if you did. She's amazing and I thank God she's mine."

"I feel the same way about your mother."

"I've always known you and Ma were two of a kind. You've made your love and respect of her known to all of us."

I looked over my father's left shoulder; Ma was taking Declan from one of her friends. He was fussing and she was quick to act. Christi was crossing the room to join her.

"Patrick, do you ever wish you'd gone after Christi when you saw her for the first time?"

I hadn't really thought about it. I didn't want to. I was just grateful I got to wake up to her beautiful face every morning.

"Honestly, I'm just glad I have all that we have now. I refuse to question the timing."

Da only nodded as he turned to watch Ma gently patting Declan's back as Christi kissed his cheek. Like a true Malloy, Declan was surrounded by women; granted, the two most beautiful were his mother and grandmother, but they were women nonetheless.

"I heard you had a talk with Dustin this week," Da spoke, changing the subject.

"Yes, I got him set up and gave him his assignments. I think he'll work out just fine."

"Of course he will. He has a purpose. Give a man a purpose and you have a man that'll work hard."

I couldn't have agreed more. My reason to live was currently standing not ten feet away with my other reason resting on her shoulder. The conversation I'd had with Mouth came to memory.

"So, is Megan's baby yours?"

"No, Mr. Malloy, but I plan to make him mine, if she'll agree." His eyes told me he spoke only the truth.

"Are you sure about that? Children aren't something you can just toss aside, not in this family, anyway."

I looked to Tonto and he nodded his head, silently giving me his word that he would make Mouth understand.

"She's my world. I know it's fast, but I can't explain it. It might make me sound like a pussy, but it's the truth. I . . . crave her."

His words spoke volumes. I knew exactly how he felt.

"I don't have to tell you that you can't tell her anything that happens in this room, correct?" Mouth only nodded his head.

"Tonto, get him fixed up with a car," I instructed as I reached into my desk and pulled out a business card. *"Give this guy a call and tell him to set you up with a decent house. Tell him you work for me and he'll know where to put you."*

Mouth took the card, placed it in his jacket pocket, then turned to leave the room.

"One more thing." Mouth stopped and turned back to me. "Mrs. Malloy wants you and Megan over for dinner this week. Don't even think about telling her no; she owns my balls, if you know what I mean."

Mouth snickered as he nodded his head. As Tonto and Mouth left the room, I clearly heard Mouth ask Tonto why I referred to him as Mouth.

I heard the sound of a hand slapping a back as Tonto replied, "Dustin, trust me when I say that you want Boss to give you a nickname. It's a sign that you're going to be family."

I guffawed as I returned to my work. Tonto was correct. I had nicknames for all of my family; well, the family that wouldn't rip off my balls for saying them out loud, anyway . . .

By the time we had retrieved Declan from all of the ladies who had attended the reception, Christi was exhausted. I loaded both of them into Christi's SUV and headed home.

It was less than two weeks later when I was awoken very early in the morning. I followed the sound and found my poor wife wrapped around the toilet, vomiting violently. I rushed to her side while she tried to shove me away.

"Patrick, you don't need to see this."

I shushed her as I ran a washcloth under the cold water and laid it along her neck. Christi was pale and her skin cold.

"Do you think it was something you ate?"

Christi turned her face in my direction and gave me a 'go to hell' look. "I highly doubt it since I'm three days late."

The smile on my face was hard to hide. Christi was as regular as they came. If she was late then that could only mean one thing.

"You're pregnant?"

"Good fucking detective work there, Sherlock," Christi tossed at me, as she leaned her head over the toilet and began to dry-heave again.

I rubbed her back and ignored her shitty attitude. We were pregnant again and nothing was going to separate us this time.

"Well, how about I run to the store and get a test?" I asked. Her body convulsed again as she continued to dry-heave over the toilet.

She lifted her left hand and pointed to the cabinet under the sink. I opened the door and sure enough, there were several home pregnancy tests and a box of tampons.

Once Christi had her vomiting under control, I left her in the bathroom to pee on the little stick. It was the longest three minutes I had ever waited through in my life. When she emerged from the bathroom with a smile, I rushed to her and hugged her tight.

"We're pregnant, Patrick. Our children will be Irish twins."

Eight months later . . .

"Christi, I know you need to push, but just hold it till I can get my gloves on."

While Christi's first pregnancy had been a breeze, this pregnancy had not. She was sick for the first four months, then had to watch her diet as she had developed gestational diabetes. Christi was a rock star, vowing to do anything to make sure this baby was healthy. The one thing that was like the first pregnancy was that she was delivering quickly.

"Okay, Christi, let's get this baby out."

Christi had called me back home not long after I'd left for work this morning. Just as I was getting her into the car, her water broke. I told her to close her eyes as I drove like a bat out of hell to get her here. Once I had her in the doors, the nurse rushed her to delivery and ten minutes later, we were about to meet our second son for the first time.

I watched Christi's face turn red and she nearly took my hand off with her grip.

"Here he is . . ."

My attention turned to the tiny pink and screaming, perfect baby who now rested on Christi's stomach. I watched as Christi took her hand and rubbed his tiny head.

"Hello, Connor, happy birthday." Christi spoke, although clearly out of breath.

"Patrick, do you want to cut the cord?" Her doctor stood at the end of the bed between my wife's legs. Her hand was extended toward me, scissors waiting for me to take. With a shaky hand, I took them, cutting the umbilical cord and severing the tie he'd had to Christi for the past nine months. I watched as they took him across the room and began to clean and weigh him.

"Eight pounds, ten ounces."

I smiled as I bent down and kissed my wife. Her hair was stuck to her forehead and I brushed it off before placing more kisses there. "Thank you," I whispered to her.

"For what?"

"For your faith in me, for giving me two perfect sons, and for saying yes."

I watched as a tear rolled down her face, I kissed it away.

"Well, then, thank you for asking me."

Her eyes were bright with love and happiness. I could only smile back knowing I put that look on her face. I loved her with every cell in my body.

"Are you ready for the next one yet?" I jokingly questioned her.

"Hell no! You keep that baby making thing away from me. I want to enjoy the two we have before we plan any more."

I could do that. As much as I loved my wife pregnant, I would give her time with our boys.

Chapter Fourteen

E VERYONE'S HEARD THE PHRASE, "KIDS say the darndest things." Christi's and my two were no exception. Mouth and Megan had fallen hard for each other. It wasn't long before he moved her and her son, Lucas, into his house. He insisted she go back to school and finish her degree. Lucas had called Mouth daddy from day one. Mouth hired a private investigator and found Lucas's biological father. He and Tonto went to visit him and convinced him to terminate his parental rights. I'd never seen a happier man than Mouth on the day he adopted Lucas. Two years later, Megan had finished her degree and they were ready to expand their family.

Since Megan wasn't Catholic, she chose to have their wedding in Ma's backyard. The ladies in our family went to work and turned the backyard into a wedding paradise, my wife's words, not mine. Abby had just turned seven and was a junior bridesmaid. Lucas and Declan were best of friends, and while Lucas walked Megan down the aisle, Declan was the ringbearer. It was during that time when children witnessed someone doing something wrong, that they felt the need to tell their parents.

Declan had insisted he and Lucas would stand beside the "big guys" during the ceremony. Christi had assured me that it wasn't a big deal as long as they behaved. Everything had gone really well with the boys until the minister said, "Do you take Megan to be your lawfully wedded wife?"

Mouth didn't even get the opportunity to respond before Declan yelled, "Mommy, that man said Auntie Megan is awful! That's not nice; he has to sit in time out."

Everyone laughed for several minutes, while Declan got very angry. I had to take him aside and explain why everyone thought that was funny.

About a year later, Christi got very sick and it just so happened to be Father's Day. I had been taking care of the boys for her and letting her rest. On that morning, however, I woke up early and couldn't go back to sleep, so I decided to get up and get some work done. I went downstairs, found that the kitchen light was on, and I could hear voices. I crept around the corner to find my two sons buck naked, flour and eggs all over the floor. They had two bowls between their legs and they were mixing the contents while they sat on the floor. When I asked them what they were doing naked on the kitchen floor, they looked me in the eye and Declan said, "Mommy doesn't let us cook unless we have play clothes on. We didn't want Mommy to get mad if we got pancakes on our pajamas." I couldn't even be mad at them. I helped them clean up the mess and together we made breakfast for Christi. That was by far one of the best Father's Days I had ever had, also because we found out Christi had been sick because she was pregnant again.

Growing up, Declan was exactly like me. Anything I did, he wanted to do. Connor, on the other hand, was a person unto his own.

He loved to read and discover things. He would catch bugs and then study them. He would watch television, not for the cartoons; he enjoyed the educational channels, such as the Discovery and History channels. Christi always encouraged him.

When Christi gave birth to Katie, the boys were none too happy to have a girl in the family. Declan said he would've rather had a new toy than a sister, and Connor, he wouldn't go anywhere near the baby. They had even asked Ma how to send her back because they didn't want a baby sister.

One afternoon, I had to stop by the house. I walked into the family room to find Declan and Connor sitting in front of the fireplace with baby Katie lying at their feet. When I questioned them as to what they were doing, they said they had sent an email to Santa and since he had worker elves, they thought he could have Katie. I took my children in my arms and explained we loved all of them, and one day they would do everything in their power to protect their little sister. We never told Christi about that one, I feared she would never sleep again.

Even though they were so young, I had no doubt they remembered my words from that day. Katie was in first grade when a little boy in Connor's class pulled her hair and then pushed her down on the playground. Connor was playing nearby and saw the entire thing happen. He called out for Declan, who helped Katie up off the ground while Connor walked over and punched the kid in the nose. Christi was called to the principal's office, she in turn called me when she learned what had happened. I took Connor to the side and had a talk with him. Many parents would have disagreed with what I told him, but he was a Malloy and he might run this family one day. I told him I was proud of him for sticking up for his little sister, however, not to go around punching people for sport.

I gave credit to Declan and Connor for making Katie the tough-as-nails woman she was today. Her brothers had no problem picking on her or teasing her, they just wouldn't let other children do it. Our children had a bond I could not possibly put into words. It was more than just protection; it was honor and courage. It had no boundaries and for them it was real.

Declan never dated anyone Connor had feelings for and the same was true for Connor. Both of my sons valued Katie's opinion when it came to the young ladies they chose. Declan's first year at college, he brought home this nice young lady, Sasha. Katie hated her from the moment she walked through the door. Declan broke up with her when they returned to school. Connor was talking to my father one Sunday afternoon about a young lady he wanted to bring to meet the family. My father assured him he was certain Christi would love her. Connor had responded, "Mom is pure of heart, she loves everyone. Katie's the one I worry about. She can see the kind of character a person really has." So when Declan brought his Katie home to meet the family, we all waited with bated breath as our Katie said hello to her. When the two Katie's hugged each other, we knew she was the one for Declan. He proposed several months later.

When Connor was seventeen, he came to my office one afternoon asking for Muscles. Muscles followed him outside and when he returned with Connor in tow, I knew something was wrong. Connor later confessed he had overheard some of the guys talking in the locker room, and the guy his sister, Katie, had gone out with the previous weekend had tried to get her to have sex with him. When she told him no, he began spreading rumors about her. Connor had decided to key the guy's car and slash his tires. He wanted the name of a good repair shop so the kid could get his car fixed. Connor had no issues paying for the damage, but he told the little punk if he tried that shit again, it would be more than his car that was damaged. I never told Connor, but I called the auto place and paid the bill. I placed the money Connor had paid in an envelope and gave it to a women's shelter.

Our children weren't always perfect little angels, far from it, actually. One event that stood out was when Declan had turned sixteen. He'd gotten in trouble at school and Christi decided that he would lose his car for two weeks. We were having dinner at my parent's house that night when my father asked Declan how he liked his car. Da had given all the grandchildren a car for their sixteenth birthday. It wasn't brand new, but it was safe and in good working order. Declan decided to spread his wings by opening his mouth that evening, a choice he would regret his entire life.

Declan answered his grandfather by saying, "Mom took away my keys, the stupid bitch." He spoke the latter under his breath, or so he thought. I didn't remember who jumped up quicker, myself or Da, but Declan suddenly found himself six inches off the floor by the collar of his shirt, with both his angry father and grandfather in his face telling him how to speak properly to the women in his life. Da was so enraged, he took the car and sold it. It was an entire year before Declan saved enough money to buy one on his own. Not a day passed after that where he didn't kiss Christi and tell her he loved her.

The moment that stood out the most in my memory didn't happen when the kids were little, it happened when our daughter was twenty-three. Ma had just found out she had breast cancer. Once the children were told, they came home and insisted on going to the hospital to see their grandmother. I watched from the door as all three of them climbed into her hospital bed and wrapped their arms around her. Katie placed a kiss to Ma's cheek and said, "Nana, when we were little, you'd always pick us up, dust us off, and ask us where we hurt. You'd kiss the spot and tell us it was all better. Tell us where it hurts,

Nana, so we can kiss it and make it better." Ma beat breast cancer. She swore it was because of the kids' kisses.

Epilogue

1 STOOD IN MY KITCHEN, tired and feeling a bit sentimental, slowly stirring my cup of tea. I closed my eyes and began to remember the happy moments that had happened in this room over the years . . .

The first morning Patrick came down those stairs, found me making him breakfast, and how he took his time thanking me. The many dinners I cooked for him and our kids. I turned to the sink and looked out into the backyard; the wooden swing set still stood as proud as the day Patrick had put it together. If those timbers of wood and steel could talk, the secrets it would reveal. The backyard where we held many birthday parties, cookouts, and Sunday afternoon football games still looked the same.

I remembered the camping trip Declan and Connor planned when they were six. They wanted to do it alone, no help from their daddy or grandpa. I smiled as I remembered them heading into the house once the sun set, they'd had enough, and wanted dinner and to watch television.

The many tea parties Katie begged her brothers to have with her and her dolls. It only took one time of Patrick joining her and from then on they sat at her table every time she asked. It wasn't until she went off to college that she was ready to part with her tea set.

The many nights Connor stood out there looking at the stars through his telescope. I thought for sure he would be an astronaut as much as that boy knew about the planets.

I moved away from the window and began walking toward the stairs. This had been a long week and I was really starting to feel it. I was finally able to relax and analyze my thoughts. As I passed the door that led to the hallway, I stopped and placed my hand on the doorframe. It was here, on the children's birthdays, we would have them stand with their backs to the frame and document their growth. I smiled as I remembered Connor and Declan running neck and neck for several years. Connor eventually won, ending up half an inch taller than Declan and Patrick.

When the kids were growing up, I always encouraged them to follow their dreams, even if it meant they didn't follow in their father's footsteps. When Declan decided he wanted to major in business, I knew he would run the family one day. Declan had a shorter fuse than Patrick and they worked for years on calming him down. When Declan brought Kate home, I knew he'd found his other half. It took a lot of sleepless nights to get her skin toughened up, though. By the time they were married, she fit right into her role. Declan became frustrated when Patrick didn't immediately turn everything over to him. He kept telling his father he was ready to be a leader, but Patrick insisted he wasn't quite ready yet.

I would always remember the day Declan had his eyes opened to the fact he still had a lot of learning to do. Thomas and Nora had been away on vacation. On the trip home, a man driving a large truck had a heart attack and died at the wheel. Unfortunately, his truck then crossed the center lane and ran head-on into their car, killing them instantly. Once Declan heard the news, he went ballistic. He wanted the family of the driver to be held accountable for his grandparents' death. Instead, Patrick did something that caused Declan to see things in a different light, changing him forever. Patrick went to the widow of the driver and gave her the money to bury her husband. Declan was a different man after that, and Patrick said he was finally ready to lead the family a few months later.

Connor was never interested in running the family. From the time he walked across that stage at his high school graduation, he set his sights on becoming a physician. When the kids would come home from college for the holidays, usually with someone in tow, Connor never did. He told me he didn't want anything or anyone to distract him.

He had just finished his residency and was interviewing with several hospitals in Chicago for a job. Having just finished a tour of yet another hospital, he decided to stop and grab a bouquet of flowers for me. He walked into the florist shop and ran into a young girl. Her name was Elizabeth and he said the moment their eyes met, he was in love. He brought her over for dinner after a month of dating her. He confided in me that he was nervous she wouldn't want to be with him when she found out what his family did. I told him to be honest with her and that I would be happy to speak with her if she had any questions. He took her out in the backyard when he told her. She laughed and said she had known from the beginning; she told him you couldn't live in Chicago and not know who and what the Malloys did. They were married two years later.

Katie was the apple of her daddy's eye. From the moment we found out she was a girl, he did everything he could to spoil her rotten. Patrick was so proud of her brothers for always protecting her. Patrick didn't know, but I was well aware of all of the fights and property damage they caused over the years. He was such a love for taking them to the store and replacing items before I discovered they were damaged. Sometimes I had wished they would have broken a few more, just so I could get an upgrade.

When Nora died, Katie asked me how the family would survive. I explained to her that we would take everything we had learned from Nana and keep the family together. Whether by accident or divine intervention, I slid easily into the role of matriarch of the family. By the time Katie had her first serious boyfriend, I was just as feared and respected as Nora had been while she was still alive.

Katie never dated anyone her brothers deemed their friends. She didn't want to cause any riffs in their circle of friends. When Frankie and Shamus married, they had a son six months later. Seamus was the most beautiful baby, with his green eyes and dark brown hair. Seamus went to a different school than Katie, so they only saw each other at family gatherings. Seamus received a football scholarship to the University of Georgia and led them to several national championships.

When he was chosen in the first-round draft picks for the NFL, he came home and asked to talk with Patrick. It seemed Seamus had harbored a long-standing crush on our Katie. He had kept his feelings hidden, thinking Katie would have to marry the man of her father's choosing. Once he felt he could take care of Katie in manner she deserved, he decided life was too short and needed to make his feelings known.

Patrick gave him permission to date Katie. When we left the two alone together, Patrick took me into the garage and wrapped his arms around me. He told me he was happy Seamus was smitten with our daughter and he hoped they would have a long and happy life together. He then kissed my neck and said he couldn't wait to chase me around the house naked again like he did before the kids came along.

Seamus was drafted by the Chicago Bears and then led them to a Super Bowl championship. During their courtship, he treated Katie like a queen. He gave her the shamrock necklace and he made it a point to keep his image clean when being seen in public with other women. Katie insisted on working as a teacher, specializing in children with learning disabilities. When Chicago won the Super Bowl, during Seamus's interview, he was asked that famous question of 'what he planned to do now that he had won the Super Bowl?' Seamus looked into the camera and asked Katie to marry him. I had watched as a single tear ran down Patrick's cheek.

Katie's wedding made Paige and Caleb's look like an afternoon tea party. Seamus had many friends and so did Katie. He took her to a private island for their honeymoon and built her a house not far from ours. Katie taught school for five years before she and Seamus decided to start a family. No one ever spoke of Seamus's mother's past; it wasn't important and Frankie was a different woman.

After Patrick officially 'retired,' he and Declan began working out together. They would run every morning and did various other fitness activities. I was thrilled as I got to enjoy the benefits. Patrick and I continued to have a very loving relationship, and despite our age, we still made love several times a week. It was nice to have the house to ourselves and we took full advantage of that, I could assure you.

Declan and Kate had a son, Aidan, and he was a carbon copy of his father. Unfortunately, Kate developed a severe case of endometriosis and had to have a hysterectomy. She cried for days after that. On the third day, I went to her house and told her to stop it. She had a loving family she needed to get herself together and quit dwelling on what she could have lost. It was then I knew Nora was still with us.

Declan had asked for help in molding Aiden into a leader for the family. Patrick, of course, puffed out his chest with pride. They worked together for several years, giving all of their years of knowledge and experience to him. Patrick went to bed each night with the assurance that his family was in good hands when his time on Earth was over.

I crawled into bed after setting my teacup on my nightstand. The bed felt cold and sterile tonight. I tucked the covers over me as I turned to my left. Patrick's pillow still had his distinct scent that had comforted me all these years. Last Monday night, we had prepared for bed as we always had. Patrick was his usual handsy self, letting me know I was in for some major loving. Patrick had always been an amazing lover and that night was no different. However, when I woke that Tuesday morning, Patrick was gone. He had died peacefully in his sleep. The smile on his face was enough to assure me he had died happy.

We buried him two days later. He now rested beside Thomas and Nora. His funeral was attended, not only by his friends and family, but by members of rival families. One came up and told me Patrick had been a fair man and would be remembered fondly.

Declan insisted I sell the house and move in with him and Katie. I refused; this was my home and I didn't want to live anywhere else. I didn't regret a single thing I had experienced during my time with Patrick, even when I had tried to divorce him. It showed me that his love for me was true and it made our bond stronger. Connor had told his guests at his wedding that he wanted a marriage that was half as happy as his parents. I believed he would have it.

I closed my eyes and ran my hand over Patrick's starched white pillowcase. He was the only man I had ever loved and the most amazing father to our children. He gave me so much during our time together, not just love and support, but heartfelt advice. Not to say we didn't fight, but the fights we did have helped to make us stronger. It cemented the cracks that others tried to wedge between us.

I kissed my fingertips and placed my hand on his pillow. My hands now wrinkled with age, my hair much more silver than red.

"I love you, Patrick," I whispered as I closed my eyes. We had told each other every night, whether we were together or apart. He would always be locked in my heart and nothing, not even death, could take that away.

I closed my eyes and drifted into a restful slumber. My eyes suddenly opened as a feeling of complete and utter peace filled my body. I rose from the bed and glanced down at my hands, gone were the wrinkles and in their place was the porcelain skin I'd had as a young girl. I crossed my bedroom to look in the mirror, only to see my wrinkles and silver hair had vanished and I looked the same as I did on my wedding day. I stared at my reflection as I raised my hand to touch my face. I smiled, my skin was once again soft and supple. I glanced back into the mirror to find a young Patrick leaning against the doorframe of our bedroom. He was dressed in linen pants and his shirt was open all the way. As I turned to face him, the room faded away and was replaced with a white sandy beach. Patrick crossed the sand and took me in his arms.

"Fancy meeting you here, Legs." His voice was as silky as ever. His hair the same as I remembered from all those years ago. I wrapped my arms around his neck and placed a soft kiss to his lips.

I looked into his deep green eyes as I said, "Patrick, forever is a long time, quit calling me Legs."

Acknowledgments

So much goes into the creation of a novel. From the first glimmer of the idea, to the outline and character development. So many factors to consider and research to be completed. Then the cover is designed and the words are made perfect by faceless professionals who take great pleasure in correcting every comma, making certain the correct name is capitalized. Then there are the readers, some devour every word, while others take their time and savor every emotion. All are important, for without one the entire journey is pointless.

I can write a million tales of love and lust, but without my editor, Elizabeth Simonton, you would not be able to understand what I am trying to convey. Once Elizabeth is finished with her infamous red pen, my battered words are bandaged and sent to another valuable person who, once again, takes my hard work and dissects it like her sixth grade science project. As hard as my job is to write my thoughts, it is hers to tell me what doesn't work and where I failed. D.J. White took my words and told me exactly where I failed, just as Elizabeth gave me commas and semicolons. D.J. gave me inspiration and solutions to the excessive and over used words. Ladies . . . I thank you.

WHERE TO FIND CAYCE POPONEA

Facebook: Shamrocks and Secrets
Twitter: @CPoponea
Email: Caycepoponea@yahoo.com

Made in the USA
Lexington, KY
20 April 2015